Delta: Rescue

ALSO BY CRISTIN HARBER

Delta: Rescue
By Cristin Harber

A MacKenzie Family Novella

Introduction by Liliana Hart

EVIL EYE
CONCEPTS

Delta: Rescue
A MacKenzie Family Novella
Copyright 2016 Cristin Harber
ISBN: 978-1-942299-35-6

Introduction copyright 2016 Liliana Hart

Published by Evil Eye Concepts, Incorporated

ACKNOWLEDGMENTS

A huge shout out to Team Titan. Thanks for the energy and excitement. I love to chat with you every day. Tackle hugs all around.

Thank you to Sharon Kay and JB Salsbury for the time spent on this project. You always find time to help and read. Love you forever.

An Introduction to the MacKenzie Family World

Dear Readers,

I'm thrilled to be able to introduce the MacKenzie Family World to you. I asked five of my favorite authors to create their own characters and put them into the world you all know and love. These amazing authors revisited Surrender, Montana, and through their imagination you'll get to meet new characters, while reuniting with some of your favorites.

These stories are hot, hot, hot—exactly what you'd expect from a MacKenzie story—and it was pure pleasure for me to read each and every one of them and see my world through someone else's eyes. They definitely did the series justice, and I hope you discover five new authors to put on your auto-buy list.

Make sure you check out *Troublemaker,* a brand new, full-length MacKenzie novel written by me. And yes, you'll get to see more glimpses of Shane before his book comes out next year.

So grab a glass of wine, pour a bubble bath, and prepare to Surrender.

Love Always,

Liliana Hart

Available now!

Trouble Maker by Liliana Hart
Rush by Robin Covington
Bullet Proof by Avery Flynn
Delta: Rescue by Cristin Harber
Deep Trouble by Kimberly Kincaid
Desire & Ice by Christopher Rice

CHAPTER ONE

Luke Brenner lived for moments when he could crush his enemies, when he could see fear as their past caught up to the present. What he had learned over the last ten years in the military and law enforcement was that men who trafficked women and drugs tended to find God when they were caught. At each takedown and arrest, someone was always pleading, always "Oh God, no" or "Oh God, help." Luke found it astonishing that just moments before, those same assholes hadn't cared who the girls were sold to or whose lives the drugs ruined. They never thought about the pain of another life stolen or what the women would be subjected to.

But Luke had.

Every day, he had. His nightmares were made of the traffickers he was about to bust. Eerily, his good dreams were quite similar—those where he escaped, where the MacKenzie Security–Delta Team joint taskforce was able to save women and sweep drugs off the Miami streets.

Well, today he intended to save some more. It'd been too long since they'd walked out with salvageable lives.

Stealthy boot steps sounded from behind, and Luke already sensed that Javier was on his six. The team was in place. This rescue op needed to be a quiet in and out, or at least an attempt to avoid mass chaos and destruction.

"We're a go," their joint-endeavor team leader, Cade MacKenzie, ordered in Luke's earpiece comm. "Execute."

"All right, all right. Let's do this." Luke nodded across the hotel hall to Grayson, who warily watched his every move.

Delta team danced on eggshells around Luke and Javier when the job dealt with traffickers. Brock Gamble, their Delta team leader, almost hadn't let Luke on this op. He could feel their concerned looks, but they needed to chill. He hadn't lost control *that* many times, and when he had, it'd been deserved. Still, the scrutiny was there.

"Damn. I'm good." *More or less.* "Calm down," he grumbled.

Gray nodded his disbelieving, pretty-boy face—as much a pretty boy as anyone could be in this type of gig. But his face was trustworthy enough that he was tasked with a simple door knock at the hotel room. They didn't want to kick down the door, and if Grayson's all-American looks kept them from doing that, fine.

Luke's face wouldn't get a door opened. Hell, if he mugged for the peephole, angry and aggressive as he was, they'd likely get into a shootout with the traffickers on the other side. Which would be fine. But Cade's orders were to take their subjects alive—not Luke's prerogative.

His blood thumped too hard. His mind raced. After today, they would be that much closer to bringing down the traffickers who had stolen and sold his girlfriend so many years ago. He wanted the Mercier cartel more than he wanted to breathe.

Knock, knock.

"We've got movement," Ryder said in the earpiece. Their sniper was in the hotel across the street with his .50 cal on point, keeping eyes on the hotel suite. "I see four women. Two men, their weapons holstered."

"Let's keep the body count down," Cade snapped.

Fuck it. Luke didn't care. If he had his way, they'd snipe the shit out of the two armed men and call the day a success. He could have a beer and disappear off the grid.

That was the advantage of being on the task force. Some higher-up bureaucrat wanted a job done and didn't mind if the rules were bent. Cade had major sway with the DEA, and Delta team, which worked under Titan Group's command, didn't mind pressing their luck with the boundaries of the law. Titan was elite. They had the know-how and reputation that put them years ahead of any other private security force. Their teams lived in a gray area that couldn't be called right or wrong—only justified.

Luke didn't mind either. He wanted to hunt. To fight. To search and investigate. He wanted to be a vigilante asshole with one purpose in life—to scour the earth for traffickers and eradicate their despicable existence.

Grayson knocked and called, "Maintenance."

A few seconds ticked by.

"No one called maintenance." The man inside sounded inherently distrustful, and that seemed about right for someone Luke wanted to kill. Their prey seemed to know his own self-preservation was in jeopardy.

Grayson chuckled in his maintenance-man character. "CO2 leak reported, buddy. Let me check before you fall asleep and die… Or not. I get paid regardless."

"Looks like they're conferring." Ryder paused from his sniper report. "Second man's picking up the phone."

"In-house call to front desk," Parker, the task force's expert IT guy, reported in their comm pieces from their offsite war room. "We're intercepting. Hang tight. Front desk, can I help you?"

Luke bounced on his toes, waiting for Parker to give the traffickers false confirmation.

"Yes, sir." Parker continued the front desk routine. "There was an issue with a faulty condenser. We're just making the rounds."

"One man heading toward the door," Ryder reported. "Second man speaking with a woman. They're all pushing into a bedroom."

The door cracked open. "Come in."

"Thanks. Figured you didn't want to die today, but what do I know?" Grayson chuckled.

As the trafficker stepped forward to check the hall, Gray grabbed his face, wrapping a hand over his mouth, then subdued him. Quickly, Javier, Grayson, and Luke entered the room, bringing the unconscious man with them.

"You're all good," Ryder said. "Three ladies on the bed. One standing. Only hostile is still unaware."

Inside the hotel room suite, Javier and Gray took both sides of the double French door leading to the bedroom, and Luke took the middle. His left hand rested on the fancy knob, his right holding the weight of his sidearm. He pushed quietly into the room and caught the eye of the standing woman. He pursed his lips together, shushing her quiet, and stuck the business end of his 9mm against the base of the man's skull. Javier and Gray went wide.

"Law enforcement. Hands in the air." Luke took the weapon from the hostile's waist and tucked it into his own. "Walk to the wall, asshole."

The man's head pivoted and lingered on the woman, then the three ladies in the bed.

"Move it." Luke's molars gnashed as irritation mixed with his adrenaline.

He grumbled but wisely relented and moved. A few steps later, he was face-first against the wall. Luke patted him down and removed an ankle-holstered .22, then bound his wrists. As planned, Javier took the man out of the bedroom, Mirandizing him as they moved him for the task force to interrogate him.

With Grayson at Luke's side, they carefully approached the women. The three on the bed were trembling as they looked at the other woman. She was dressed differently. If he knew the Mercier cartel, that woman had been cleaned up and was about to hit the market. She was wearing a dress and had on makeup. The joint team had arrived in time to save her. One more life they'd been able to salvage.

"Relax." He approached cautiously. "We're the good guys. We're getting you out of here."

None of them spoke, and he could almost smell their fear and distrust.

"It's okay," Grayson tried. His voice offered a reassurance that Luke's couldn't.

"How did you find us?" asked the standing woman with a hint of an unfamiliar accent and a confidence that didn't match the situation. Her soft features stood out against the aged years in her eyes. Who knew who she was in real life—traffickers didn't care who they stole, college students or CEOs—and who knew what she had seen while they had her, but it had to have been a lot. This woman—nearly his age, maybe—had witnessed hell. But her shoulders were back, and she had the distrusting spirit of a fighter, which Luke admired.

"We're help," he offered.

A woman on the bed shifted. "But—" Then she cut herself off as the three others turned toward her in harsh surprise—or fear. What didn't the task force know? What couldn't they see?

"You're letting us go?" The standing woman stepped closer to the bed.

"Not immediately." Luke shook his head briefly. "It's best if you come with us first."

She pursed her full lips. "I don't want to."

"Ladies?" Grayson ignored her and spoke to the three on the bed. "We'll get you safe."

As they eagerly nodded their heads, Luke could've sworn a flicker of uncertainty and curiosity darkened the woman's face. He stepped closer to her, noting that the three on the bed looked well taken care of, considering. "What's your name?"

"What's yours?" she countered.

"Brenner." His eyes narrowed, and surprisingly, he had to bite down a smile because while she was feisty, she was also in danger. Amusement was poor form given the circumstances, and she was a victim. "Luke Brenner. What do you say we get you out of here? We'll deal with the men who took you."

Her flat lips pursed. "I don't need your help. If I'm free to go—"

"Easy. Promise, we'll take care of you."

Her eyes flared, and color hit her cheeks. "I don't need it."

Grayson cleared his throat. "We doing this?"

"Yeah." Luke moved forward, ushering the girls off the bed. "Let's move before someone else arrives."

"Where are you from?" the woman asked again, this time with more strength.

"Nowhere." No need to get into the politics of where everyone was recruited for the task force.

"No," she pressed him. "You're not local."

"And you're from here?"

Her accent was nothing he was familiar with. Javier's Brazilian accent and Ryder's Aussie drawl were easy to decipher. Not so hers, which sounded smooth, almost like hidden elegance, and the cadence made him pay closer attention.

"I asked you first," she said.

He turned back toward her. "I have a job to do. Let's move boots."

"Same. Let me walk away. I want to go home and forget about all of this."

He lowered his voice. "Did they touch you? Hurt you?"

Her chin jutted up. "*No.* Not all of them are like that."

"Yeah, I'll bet. What's your name?"

She tilted her head toward him, then caught the eyes of the other girls. "If we talk to you, they'll find us. They'll kill us. That's the truth. Better to know that now than regret it later."

Luke stepped between her and the other women. "Come in to headquarters. We'll work it out."

The women shifted uneasily. The tension in the room crept higher, and the reasons were unclear.

"What?" he asked.

She pivoted her gaze around him to the bed. "You don't know them like I do. If we talk, we will die."

"Take it easy," Grayson broke in. "Let's get out of here. We'll figure out how to keep everyone safe."

"They'll never forget." Her dark hair fell over her shoulders as she shook her head. "Never. Not if we talk. Let everyone leave. That's best. Like we escaped."

Luke took a step forward. "What I'm telling you is that we *need* to go, and eventually, you'll be able to trust me."

She leveled him with a stare so cold, so hot, so absurdly confusing, that he took a step back. "I trust no one."

"We're out." Grayson guided the other girls from the hotel room. "Get a move on, buddy."

The woman rolled her lips and stared. Their standoff couldn't go on much longer. No telling if Cade would call in backup or if the traffickers had security triggers already in motion. Luke *could*—maybe *should*—pick her up, throw her over his shoulder, and be on his merry fuckin' way. But hesitation had frozen him, staring at one of the most beautiful women he'd ever encountered.

"My name is Luke Brenner. I'm the guy you have to trust. Badge." He flicked his waist. "Team." His chest. "I'm the good guy. I'll help you sort out what you need to. But we need to leave."

She didn't move a muscle. "You don't know what you're doing."

"The same could be said for you."

Her dark eyes narrowed. "I'd like to leave on my own."

"We have to ask you a few questions."

"Ask now then let me go." She wasn't scared, wasn't cocky. An enigma more complicated than a simple victimization.

"Again. What's your name?"

Defiance danced on her lips. "It doesn't matter."

"Look, lady. I'm not going to hurt you."

Her eyes ran up his body, sizing him up, and finally landing on his face. "You look like you do nothing but hurt people."

"Only the bad ones."

"There are shades of bad." For a flash of a second, he saw the victim, the scared woman who didn't have a choice. But that faded in an instant as she sighed, seemingly letting her guard down. "Fine. I'll go with you, but I need to use the bathroom."

"Now?" He shifted in his boots, the urge to drag her out overpowering his manners.

"Please."

"Shit," Cade murmured in Luke's earpiece. "Two minutes. Get her out of the building in less than two minutes. Read me?"

He nodded agreement for Ryder to report in to the task force's commander, but the woman took his nod as permission to hit the bathroom. Before he could say anything, she hurried away. The red soles of her expensive-looking shoes caught his eye, and something felt wrong about the girl. His thoughts went into overdrive. Who was she sold to? How long had they had her? Did she worry this was a cartel test where the traffickers tested their women to see if they'd run? Did she know her new owners?

"Hey, boss. What do we know about—"

Muffled glass shattered from the bathroom. Luke spun and slammed against the locked door.

"What—" Ryder broke into his thoughts via his earpiece. "—the fuck? Your girl's pulling herself through a tiny-ass window."

With another slam against the bathroom door, it broke open. Luke's eyes peered out the tiny, broken window.

"We've got a problem." Grayson's voice crackled through the

earpiece as Luke stood in disbelief in the empty bathroom.

Ryder broke in. "She's scaling the damn wall, climbing toward a balcony."

"*What?*" Luke's mind spun.

"These girls," Grayson said, "say that lady is management. *Upper* management."

His blood went cold. *She* was a goddamn human trafficker? Luke jumped onto the toilet and peered past the broken glass.

"I've got a shot," Ryder announced. "You want management taken out?"

"No!" he snapped, against everything he had stood for in his life. "No shot."

"No," Cade agreed, less forcefully and more calculating. "Where's she going?"

"Roof," Ryder replied. "Seventh floor. She's climbing toward the roof."

Luke took off, barreling through the hotel room and gunning it for the hotel's staircase. Did he just say no to shooting a human trafficker? They *all* needed to be taken out, even the pretty ones with full lips and innocent faces. But something was missing. No way could she be involved in this. Even as he took three stairs at a time in a full sprint, he wanted to see with his eyes if it were true.

The hotel was twelve stories tall. Part of him worried that she'd kill herself accidentally before he could catch her.

"Update, Ryder," he said.

"Woman's still moving. Kicked off her shoes and hauling ass."

"Son of a bitch. Where now?"

"Eleven."

Same as him.

"We have company." Ryder's vocal inflection was concerned.

"Hold back, Brenner." Cade jumped in. "Read me, Luke?"

At the roof door, he didn't want to stay back. "Why?"

"Asshole. You do not question. You listen."

Damn it. "Who's out there?"

"Brother," Ryder broke in, "we have a chopper coming in fast, rifleman hanging out the opening."

"Fuck!" Luke slammed both hands on the door.

"Stay put!" Cade ordered.

Ryder layered in. "They'd take you out in a heartbeat."

"She's out there?" Luke asked.

"Roger. Estimated ETA for a pickup, fifteen seconds."

Fuck it. Cade can kick my ass later. Luke pushed through the door and ducked defensively into the humid heat, pressing against the wall to take in his surroundings. There. The object of his unfathomable interest hustled across the south side of the roof. "Hold up! Stop."

She spun, eyes wild, out of breath from their adrenaline-filled race.

Luke bunched his fists, holding himself back, more curious, or even turned on, than sane at the moment.

"Who the fuck are you?" he shouted.

Their eyes locked. The chopper lowered, and not wanting to die that day, he threw his hands up and hoped it enough to keep himself from being target practice. They'd still shoot, he'd still die. Ignoring his orders and entering the rooftop was a huge mistake, but he needed to know who she was. His reasoning had abdicated authority, and she was the unknowing catalyst.

"I'm going to find you," he said.

A ladder dropped from the helo. She quickly grabbed onto it, shouting what he guessed was an instruction *not* to shoot.

Why? Why would she say that? They were enemies. They survived because the other one didn't.

But as he wondered, an arm reached out of the helo and pulled her inside. She was safe from falling, safe from Ryder's sniper rounds, and that was a relief, which screwed with his head more than her scaling a Miami hotel. The chopper pulled back hard and fled. Task force intel buzzed in his ear, communicating that a satellite had locked onto the bird. Parker would work his magic and see where it ended up. Simple. Their team would get them. Eventually.

Still, Luke stood there with too many questions. Namely, who *was* that girl? And for the first time, he wanted answers as much as he wanted blood.

CHAPTER TWO

Pulling out his earpiece to silence his cursing team leader, Luke pushed back inside to the air-conditioned hall and bounded down the stairs. When he hit the ground floor, Javier and Ryder were waiting. Grayson and the girls were gone. Luke's chest hammered, and his mind couldn't latch on to a logical course of action, so he stayed silent and fell into place when they boarded their blacked-out Expedition.

"Where's Cade?" Luke asked.

Ryder shook his head. "Rode back with Gray."

Luke nodded. He had about five minutes of quiet before they showed at their rendezvous, where Cade would tear him a new asshole.

"Damn it." He tried to contain the hum of his muscles. Stress exacerbated that uncontrollable urge for pain. To inflict it. To receive it. He wasn't a sadist—just a fighter. And clenching his fists only to release and do it again, he felt a growing need to find a brawl.

"What happened up there?" Javier slowed, already exiting the highway onto a palm-tree-lined street decorated with brilliantly painted buildings. A co-op grocery, local restaurants, housing that had seen better days. The farther they drove, the sketchier the area, until they were in a place Delta and MacKenzie security could hide unnoticed.

"Dunno, Brazil." Luke rubbed his eyes, hunched over in his seat. "Things happen."

"I get it. If anyone gets it, *I* get it. But…shit." Javier whistled. "Cade's gonna light you up."

"I know."

Ryder clapped Luke on the back as they pulled into the parking lot. Javier threw the SUV into park, and Luke looked up, wondering if his screw-up would kick him off the team.

"Ready?"

"Fuck if I care." Which was a total lie. He wanted cartel blood. He wanted to know about the girl.

"Right." Ryder got out.

Luke dropped his head back and heard Javier say, "Shit happens. We'll get them another day."

They would. Both he and Javier needed that to be the truth. They might have different trafficking targets, but they thought the same way, lived for the same goals. Luke grumbled and opened the door.

Cade stood a dozen yards away. "Let's go, asshole."

Fuck it. He fell in step, and they walked into an abandoned garage that Cade had taken over as a home base for the past few days. Hot air hung heavy with the scent of expired oil and brake dust from years before.

"Didn't have your ears on?" Cade asked.

Luke flicked the abandoned earpiece off his shoulder. "You know I did."

"So no excuses then. Not listening for what purpose? I don't have time to babysit your dumb ass, you get that. Brock sent you down here with a giant fucking warning. You screw up, you're off the job. I don't want a body count that includes anyone on my team. I have a damn reason when I say stay on the sidelines. Do you get that?"

He nodded. "Yeah."

"You don't come from a background where you've been broken down and built up, but you better fucking believe that's what I'll do if you can't listen and follow orders. Do you understand?"

He shrugged and was slammed against the wall so quickly he almost didn't see it coming.

Cade thrust into his face, their eyes inches apart. "You want me to destroy you? You want to know what the bottom of my fuckin' boots tastes like?"

"No."

"Good. Get your head out of your ass and stay on point." Cade stepped away, shaking his head. But he looked back because they both knew what had to come next.

Some folks drank, others a lot worse. Luke needed the pain.

"Get the fuck out of here, and don't get your ass arrested," Cade said.

That was all it took—their agreement, which Brock had negotiated with Cade. Luke would fight when he needed to. He'd take part in that blessed addiction that kept his head sane. He nodded and went to drop his gear and change out of what kept him safe—the gear, the Kevlar, the guns and knives. He wanted to forget it all just long enough to go find a fight and have nothing to protect him but his speed and agility. Sometimes Javier accompanied him—they had the same mindset about the saving grace of brawling—but not today.

Luke didn't say good-bye as he pushed out the door, walking who knew where. Miami always provided a way to alleviate the pressure, whether it was an organized throw down or just a picked fight. By the time the night was done, *management* would be a distant figure in his memory, and his focus would be on his end goal. Eradication.

* * * *

The Mercier corporate office in downtown Miami was a façade. Maddy hated the desk, hated the job, and would much rather have been at *her* company, Love, Inc. She had two jobs, two lives. They were interconnected, but Mercier was the opposite of Love.

She despised Mercier almost as much as she did her father, who owned the sketchy conglomerate and source of his wealth that made him richer than sin. Some girls wanted to meet a billionaire and be whisked away, but not Maddy. She knew too many of the men who had as much money as her family. None had made it in a way that they should. None spent their dollars on decent activities.

And *all* spent their money on pleasure.

Pleasure was something she didn't understand...at least the sexual kind. Pretty people, beautiful clothes, and a sunset over the beach were simple things that brought her pleasure.

Her mind raced back to earlier. The law enforcement team she'd escaped had DEA emblazoned on their fronts or badged on their hips. Even if Maddy thought her father was neck-deep in trafficking, she only thought he moved women—not that drugs weren't as bad or worse. But it might be that he was expanding. Her stomach sank. All this time spent to get to the heart of Mercier Corporation, and she missed that?

What good was she as a Trojan horse if she didn't know the extent of what she wanted to destroy?

The desk phone chirped before her secretary's voice filtered through the speaker. "Ms. Mercier, your father is on the line."

Maddy glared at her phone but answered as she always did, her muscles aching from the exertion of her escape. She might have been trained, but she didn't have to escape and evade in the normal course of her life—though it had happened occasionally before working with the slime Mercier dealt with.

One day, she would take down Mercier and make Love, Inc. her only focus. *After* she destroyed everything her father stood for. "Yes, Papa?"

"I need you to inspect a new shipment. It will arrive to replace the merchandise we lost."

The merchandise he lost? Meaning the *women* who were saved by American law enforcement, a group of agents who didn't take Mercier money? She almost hadn't thought those people existed.

Her father was evil, but was she much better? Mercier was the family business, the only existence she knew. For as long as she could remember, growing up, she'd been sequestered on their estate in the south of France. This was the life she knew. Papa's business trade partners and her tutors came in and out of the house to give her an English education and erase her French accent. She knew no other children but her brother, knew no other life, nor a mother. Yet somehow she knew the business that she and Lucien, her brother, were being groomed for was wrong. Maybe that counted for something, that she wasn't inherently evil, just completely messed up in the head—ruined as a woman before she ever had an interest in being feminine. She found it ironic that the family business sold sex—and now likely drugs—yet she was a virgin with not a single smidge of interest in sex.

Many times she'd come to the conclusion that she lacked the gene that would allow her to experience desire. That was punishment for her involvement with Mercier.

Still, she was there. Papa had even helped set up her successful business in Miami. Maddy was talented, with a keen eye for business. After all, she'd had the best business education his money could buy. Love, Inc. was a modeling and scouting company. While Papa saw it as something for her to do to handle the boredom that would come from living in a place as distasteful as Miami and overseeing Mercier corporate offices, she needed Love, Inc.'s income to support her long after she brought down her father.

Between Mercier and scouting for Love, she had her fingers in so many parts of underground Miami that she didn't know whether to hate herself or be proud. Either way, the life she led had colored a part of her soul, one of many reasons she couldn't feel anything on the inside.

God, she was screwed up in the head.

Papa needed her to assess what product to keep or, worse, what to sell. Rather…who to sell. Once they were gone, they were gone—slaves to their masters, whores to their pimps. No matter what happened to the sold merchandise, their salvation was impossible. At least right now.

"Madeleine?"

She swallowed away the urge to vomit or scream her rejection. "*Oui*, of course."

"Let's see what we have." Papers rustled in the background.

This was nothing but a business transaction. He was likely looking at their invoices and would expect a full report from Maddy. They diversified their product line, selling as many women into whorehouses as they did wealthy fetish deviants.

"Seven new girls."

"*Sept?*" The French rolled off her tongue as she cringed, hoping her surprise and disgust didn't bleed through the call. Long ago, she'd thought about calling the authorities, both at home and in America, but it seemed that even law enforcement was Papa's friend or on his payroll. She didn't know enough about the legal side of life to trust it. Nor did she want to end up in prison. She suspected that was the reason her curiosity was so stoked after having escaped the hotel room raid.

Maybe Mercier's fall was less of a daydream when men like the American agents really existed. She bit her lip, not wanting to get her hopes up, not trusting the tinge of excitement percolating in her chest.

Trust no one. Expect betrayal. Always have a plan to escape. Those were her father's words, which had been trained into her for as long as she could remember.

Papa would one day die. He was protected night and day, so she couldn't help the process along. Murdering her father...? Maybe she *was* as evil as him.

"Yes. Seven." More papers rustled. "You cost the company money today. Three girls removed into US custody? Two of my men?" He tsked into the phone.

Her head dropped, the battle between guilt and anger raging. "Yes, sir."

"Tell me. When our men talk to the police, are they going to mention why there weren't the five girls in the hotel room? Four and you. I believe there was one missing. Because US agents only took *three* girls into custody."

Her stomach dropped. The other girl was a waste of a sex slave. She wouldn't have held up mentally, physically. She'd had too much trauma before ending up in Maddy's care. So she'd done the only humane thing—bought the girl herself and let her go. Fake papers. A new identity. And a doctor who would help her come back from the brink. But all of that, no one could know. If she could do it for every girl, she would. *Soon...*

"See, Papa, I thought—"

"Madeleine," he snapped. "You've been caught before, and you promised those days of bleeding-heart help were over. This is a *business*. You understand that?"

"Yes, sir."

He grumbled. "If they had any intelligence on the female count today, you are lucky they considered you the fourth, not part of

Mercier."

"Yes, sir." Her eyes pinched closed, and not for the first time, she realized why her father had had her French accent wiped from her English education. He knew, even when she was a child, this would be her life. "I only meant to—"

"I don't want to hear it."

"No one would want her." She dropped her head, making her shoulders ache, and balled her fists. She ignored her sore fingers, wishing she had something her father wouldn't refute.

"Someone will always want what we have. You know this."

The truth hurt. "Yes, sir."

The market was filled with high-end buyers as well as the ones who wanted scraps. Scrappers reminded her of the fighters in Miami's underground, the bottom feeders who knew no other life. But amid the scum and dregs of society, she also saw the champions, the athletes, the specimens of raw talent. She loved the brawls and bankrolled several off-the-books brawls, sponsoring the fighters who loved the pain and the egos who didn't know they should walk away. Watching the dynamics of that world was her entertainment. Some people watched TV and movies. She enjoyed the dark side of life where people made their own choices and no one was put on sale by another.

"Okay, my girl. Check the new merchandise and make the numbers work in our favor."

"Yes, sir." Her head back in the conversation, '*Yes, sir*' was all she could say to Papa.

The line went as dead as her soul felt after those calls with Papa. The girls—his new *females*—were her age more often than not, late teens, early twenties, though she lived as though she was three times her real age. Living this life made her insides dark and empty.

Her brother had been a sick deviant. The horrors they had seen at their estate, the echoes of awfulness that they'd heard while growing up, all of that had made Lucien aroused—just like her father. Lucien should've been the next leader of the family business, but he'd had an *accident*. To this day, she wondered how he really died.

But if he had been alive, then she wouldn't have her

opportunity to make things right as best she could. That was her reason for living, even if she was doing things that made her want to die along with her brother.

Maddy pulled up a screen on her computer and cried on the inside. One day, she would be in a place to destroy Mercier, but until then, she was a businesswoman and a part of one of the most powerful brokerages of human beings. And that broke her heart.

CHAPTER THREE

Luke's eyes cracked open, letting the break of day ease him awake. He'd been on the job in Miami for two weeks and slept only two nights' worth. So when he finally got home to Ft. Worth, he went to bed and stayed there. At least a day or two of straight sleep had passed, and hunger and daybreak were calling.

He rubbed his knuckles into his eyes then jumped out of bed and hit the floor. He ran through his regimen. A hundred sit-ups. A hundred push-ups. Two large glasses of water. Then he could start his day.

A protein bar made up his breakfast, and it was almost gone when his phone rang. MacKenzie Security and Delta Team were the only ones that had that number. If it was ringing, that meant work. Good, because he'd had just about enough downtime.

"Yeah?"

"There's new intel. We're digging into those trafficking fuckers again." Cade's growl made him take notice. "Brock says you're good to go."

"I'm ready," Luke said. Saving women, sweeping drugs, and dismantling traffickers were what he lived for.

"Good. We're pulling together the plan now. What we know is the son of a rival cartel is in Miami, apparently unhappy with a business transaction with Mercier. We've had eyes on him for a while. Chatter from our sources says that they plan to hit close to home. The how and when we're working on."

"All right." He bunched his fists and cracked his knuckles.

"Look, Luke." Cade cleared his throat. "If we're right, he's the one you've been looking for."

Wait... "The one?""

Cade grunted. "Looks like."

"If you're shitting me..."

"Suit up. Head back to Miami. Rendezvous location to be provided."

Luke let out a shaky breath, nerves and anticipation warring within. How would this play out? Could he find the asshole who had taken his girlfriend so many years ago? No peace would ever come from it. Too many years had passed, and surely she was long gone. His only prayer was she went quickly, not having to suffer. However, the man who bought her and the men who facilitated her auction? They would suffer at Luke's hands, even if he had to take them out one by one. That was the only thing he wanted in life. *Redemption.*

He dropped the protein bar wrapper on the counter of the rent-by-a-week apartment and grabbed his go bag, ready to head to Miami and knock off a to-do item on his retaliation list.

* * * *

Love, Inc. was nothing if not proficient. Maddy powered through to her office with a perfect smile, a sexy wrap dress, and flawless hair. She looked the part—*everything* looked the part—and when she was there, she felt it too.

Models were eerily similar to the women Mercier sold. The business was run almost exclusively on referral for both clients and talent.

Her phone rang as she sank into the buttery leather of her executive office chair. Answering the call, she looked out her window onto Miami's orange-and-red sunset. "Yes, hello?"

"I'm so sorry." The voice whimpered. "I messed up."

A chill ran down her spine. "Lori? Is that you?"

Lori was one of her models, always looking for a way to hit the big leagues before she was ready. "I took a shoot off the books. Really, I'm so sorry. I was wrong. It wasn't—" A raspy breath echoed through the phone. "I need a doctor. He—" A sob sent another chill down Maddy's spine. "Hurt me. I'm so sorry." Lori's voice, hoarse and tear soaked, rang in Maddy's ears.

"Lori, sweetheart. Where are you?"

"Where the Calvin Vine shoot was yesterday." She sobbed. "I thought he was part of them. I thought—"

"Doesn't matter, sweetie. Help is coming for you. Are you safe now?"

"Yes," she whispered hoarsely.

"You'll either see me, Hale, or the cops very soon." However, any interaction with Miami's finest always made her nervous.

"Thank you."

Maddy ended the call, then dialed the head of Love's security detail. "Hale, Lori took a job off the books. It went all wrong. I think she was attacked. Get there to help with the cops *and* give me a name. I want him before they get him."

"Damn it," he growled. "On it. Where is she?"

She pulled up the schedule to find the Calvin Vine location from the day before, anger forcing her to focus on the next move. Incidents like that rarely happened. She screened her clients, staff, and model roster well. The industry was never one hundred percent safe, though she offered the girls the best possible chance of safety in a business that was filled with sleazy photogs, eating disorders, and drugs, which her father was apparently selling. Still, when something bad happened, especially what she thought might've happened to Lori, Maddy wanted swift, brutal payback.

"Hotel Miranda," she said.

"All right. I'm two minutes out."

"Good…and Hale?"

"Yes, ma'am."

"Lori is strong." Maddy's French accent tinged her English when she was angry, and she was fuming. "But if she was brutalized, care for her as best you can. She will fight it but need it."

"Understood."

Hale was American ex–special forces. Ex because they'd kicked him out. He had a problem turning his hostility down when he needed to. He had been hired by her father as her bodyguard when she first came to Miami. Hale was not stupid and quickly saw through the Mercier façade, but he needed the paycheck. As time went along, he was the only person who knew her on the inside and outside, knew what she was and where she wanted to go. When Love came into existence, he transitioned from her personal detail to run the security shop.

They'd never been romantically involved, primarily because she was unable to tap into that part of her psyche, which seemed completely broken. But he cared for her, much like she imagined a brother would if he weren't a sicko like her Lucien.

Whenever Hale went on a job like that, he was ruthless, but only after he'd handled Maddy's model with expert care. There was no question that he would track down who did this before the cops, and revenge would be swift.

Taking a deep breath, Maddy opened a desk drawer. She might send Hale to lead the hunt, but she would be involved too. No one hurt her girls without having to face her. If there was one benefit from being Papa's daughter and seeing the Mercier empire at work her entire life, it was that she knew how to exact payback. Waiting patiently for use was her favorite .22.

✦ ✦ ✦ ✦

Lori had been hurt every way a woman could be hurt. Anger thumped in Maddy's neck as she left the girl's side. Even the doctor, who was no stranger to various questionable industries, was affected by what happened to Lori. Maddy's rage was near blinding, but she controlled it and left as the cops began probing the *who*s and *why*s of what happened.

Hale followed behind her as she retreated, leaving Lori in the care of a close friend on the way to the hospital.

When they were both streetside and she couldn't contain the need to scream, Maddy turned to him. "Hale—"

"I know who it is."

"That fast?"

"He's *connected*."

God. "To Mercier?"

Hale nodded. "Yes."

"Damn it! Those disgusting—"

"I've pinpointed him. He knows who you are, and I'd guess

this is a message to your father."

Of all the people walking the earth, Hale understood why she wanted to kill Papa. The local cops, the feds, and Interpol were no match for her father. He had ins everywhere: Miami, Abu Dhabi, Madrid, Hong Kong. *Everywhere.* No agency existed that could do what she needed to. But her process was slow.

"Maddy? He'll hear from someone else if you don't tell him first."

"Whoever hurt Lori is mine. Not Papa's. Before you teach him a lesson, before we hand him over to the police, *he is mine.*"

He gave her a lecturing, hardened glare but acquiesced. "Yes, ma'am."

"Address."

"Not too far." He gave it to her as they swiftly moved from the swanky Hotel Miranda. "I'm riding with you."

"Not tonight, you aren't." She smiled at the valet, who went to retrieve her sports car. "Hale, get in your own ride and give me a ten-minute head start."

"Maddy—"

She flashed him a look as the sleek black Lotus pulled up. According to Papa, being discreet didn't mean avoiding cars priced as much as housing. He preached looking the part. He was a CEO, and she was an executive. He ran a trillion-dollar company, and she was on its board and was also the head of one of the fastest-growing modeling agencies in the world. So a Lotus it was. Other than material extravagance, they were tight-lipped and well hidden.

"Ms. Mercier," the attendant said as he held the door for her. The staff were more than familiar with her and her models, who often traipsed in for couture events. Sometimes she thought the staff guessed that the high-end modeling agency was a front for Mercier's dealings, but that didn't matter, at least not tonight.

"Thank you." She turned to Hale before sliding into the leather seat. "Ten-minute head start."

He shook his head. "I can't let you do that."

"Hale—"

"*Maddy.* If your father finds out—"

"Let him." Her brow furrowed because she knew he was right and she wasn't thinking clearly. A .22 in her purse wasn't much of a defense against the man who had sadistically hurt Lori—not unless Maddy walked in and just shot him, and if her father did find out that she'd purposefully kept a message from him, even for a limited amount of time, the man she was about to hunt wouldn't be her problem.

"Think about what you're doing." Hale stepped closer.

Retaining some of her composure, she tilted her head and motioned him into the passenger seat. "Let's go."

Already walking to the opposite side of the car, he pressed his cell phone to his ear, no doubt doing what she paid him well to do—protect her and ready their team to avenge her girl.

He programmed a location into the GPS. The directions took her to a seedy, though not poor, section of the city. The area wasn't safe, but that wasn't a concern. That was the part of town she frequented that had nothing to do with her models.

"Why's this guy staying in a shithole like this?" she asked.

Hale shook his head. "No idea."

Most who frequented that area knew her, or if they didn't personally, they knew of her. God had been kind to her in the looks and brains departments, and she'd worked hard to create Love. But that wasn't what made her a local underground legend—it was her temper, the protective wrath she had when it came to her models, her business, or even the underground side businesses she tinkered with. Everyone knew they were to be untouched.

All her hired muscle were as loyal as they were clued in. They knew that underneath the thousand-dollar shoes and designer dresses, Maddy was a beast raised by a monster, every day reminding the world that looks were deceiving.

She blew out an anticipatory breath and double-parked on the street. "This is it?"

Hale was already pushing out of his seat, and that was all the confirmation she needed. She caught sight of two of their men's vehicles parked under the sun-setting shade of a low-leaning palm. Their team was already there. Leaving her purse but taking the .22, she left the Lotus unlocked, and God help anyone who tried to take her ride. Then she strode toward the building.

Hale was paces ahead of her, but he slowed and turned at the front of the walk. "Easy in there, Maddy."

She raised a brow. "What part of what we just saw says I should be easy?"

His eyes darkened. "I'm just asking for you to let me do the dirty."

"We'll see."

After climbing the well-worn stairs, they reached the unit with weathered blue paint, and she turned the door handle. Ahead of her sat the piece of shit, gagged, tied to a chair, hands and legs bound, and two of her men were posted against the bright-yellow wall. Cockiness colored the bound man's eyes where she wanted to see fear. When he focused on her, that didn't change. It should have. It would soon enough.

"Ungag him." She paced. "And back the chair to the wall."

Hale obeyed.

She spun on a heel, deliberately toying with the weapon in her hand. "Tell me about you."

The man cackled. "Tell me about your father."

"Wrong answer." Maddy nodded.

Hale's brass-knuckle-clad fist socked the guy, snapping his head against the wall.

"He's just warming you up for me. I'm worse. I'm your nightmare, and before I turn you back over to my boys, you deal with me."

Hale growled. "His name is Felipe Rivera."

Felipe's eyes tightened at the name, but nothing came out of his mouth.

"Well, Felipe." She inched closer. "Any apology you wish to give?"

"Your whore was hurt—"

"Model," Maddy corrected.

"Whatever you wish to call her," he continued. "Make sure your father knows the Riveras were close enough to hurt your business, hurt you."

The asshole was trying to hurt the unfeeling with the innocent. "You took my girl in the mouth when she said no? That was a mistake. Hit her, hurt her? You will feel that too." She stepped toward him, standing knee to knee with the tied man. "You stole her body without her permission? Made her bleed?"

With that, the man shifted, jutting his chin as though offering a *fuck you* to her father.

"You're going to beg"—she leaned forward to his ear—"and plead to be put down like the dog you are. But I won't let you die." She nudged her knee to his. "I'm a teacher. You will learn."

As she turned toward Hale, the door crashed open, and something heavy thumped on the floor. Her heart pumped as the flashbang exploded. Its pop was louder than the door had been, and the quick smoke-spitting bomb hissed. Trained instinct kicked in. Never show fear, always have an escape, but she didn't see her options. Commandos burst into the room, one to the right, the next to the left. A third man stood by the door while another remained outside. Panic soared in Maddy's racing blood, and her stinging eyes leaked tears.

The commotion threw her team into play, but she stood there, unflappable amid the shouts and the smoke, never showing fear, always facing her enemy until she could survive.

Hale yelled, "Stand down!"

Other voices ordered them to do the same. The chaotic clash spun around her, but she didn't waver. Bring on the law. Let them try to take her down. She had no fear when she was high on adrenaline.

"Down!" Hale ordered. "Down, down. Get the fuck down, Maddy."

No.

Boots were stomping into the room, men shouting. Her security was ready for war. No weapons had been fired, but no one knew what the next move was.

"North wall." One of the commandos reported their mark, her captive, tied to a chair. "Confirmation on Rivera."

In all the craziness, she put her hands on her hips. "Enough." Nothing changed as a man surged toward Rivera. She moved in front of him and dropped her chin, shouting with all the anger that Lori deserved, "Enough!"

That time, the room stilled. The man in front of her froze. Hale and a man attacking him, hands still on each other, stopped. Everyone noticed that she was a she, not throwing swings like in an action movie—everyone except for one.

He marched over, got in her face, and growled, "On the bed, facedown."

Her hand flew to slap his face. He wore tactical gear: hat, goggles, and body armor. But his cheek was bare, and her slap left a mark on his sculpted chin. He didn't flinch, and he stood stoic and statuesque, towering over her like a military mafia man.

"Stand down," he told her in a voice all too familiar.

Letting her eyes drift down, her curiosity was piqued amid the bodies and lingering smoke. *DEA* was branded on his chest.

Luke Brenner—twice in recent history?

But that didn't matter. The bastard in the chair was hers. After what had happened to Lori, Maddy didn't care who this team was or what they wanted. She even ignored her fear of the law. Retaliation was the only option—Luke and friends had to leave.

She pursed her lips. "No."

"One last time." His words rolled over her senses. Even in the midst of the tension and chaos, she noticed how masculine it was, making her flash back to the hotel from weeks before. "Back down."

This was a challenge she wouldn't back down from, whether she was curious about this ops team or not. "Rivera's mine. Walk away."

"What are you doing here?" Menace gripped his question. "We know who you are. Mercier management."

"Wrong." At the moment, she wasn't, nor would she admit to that outside a corporate boardroom or press function. "I'm a nameless, faceless solution to a piece-of-crap problem."

"You should be in cuffs."

She squared her shoulders, angry to have lost control of what she wanted and losing control of herself because of it. "It's *never* going to happen."

"Lady, we have jurisdiction, a search warrant, and *you* interfering with an investigation. *You*, who we have seen before and should bring the hell in."

Hale cleared his throat, stepping toward her. "Ma'am."

"Come on in," Luke urged, "since the last time we didn't finish our conversation."

"No," Hale answered for her.

A tickle of realization broke through her fury at the man who'd hurt Lori. Self-preservation kicked in at the thought of Luke cuffing her and hauling her in for questioning—not a good situation. Papa's anger would cause problems and slow her ultimate plan for a takeover. Grinding her teeth, she backed down. "We were just leaving." But then she turned to Felipe Rivera. "I'm not finished with you. No matter where they take you, what they do to you, I will find you."

With that, she turned on her heel and walked straight to the door, letting the armed men in front of her part as her team followed her footsteps. No one tried to stop her—not a single question—which was interesting if for no other reason than the men in the room hadn't wanted to let her go before.

CHAPTER FOUR

Luke pivoted, watching the woman walk out. His dick was rock hard, and his blood pounded in his lungs. Around him, the team bustled into action. She was Mercier management, and he was letting her fucking walk. In what world did that happen? But they weren't here for her, and the Rivera cartel was the one responsible for his girlfriend's disappearance years before. *That* was his guiding focus, not that lady, not Mercier. Only the memory of his old girlfriend.

Cade marched in. "What the fuck happened?"

"Rivera had company."

"I see that. And they *left?*"

"Didn't come here for them—"

A growling hiss came from the tied-up Felipe Rivera. "That lady is psycho. Untie my hands. Get me out of here!"

Everything in Luke changed. His blood morphed from pounding to boiling. Anger exploded in his mind. "We are not your saviors."

"Time to roll," Cade reminded him. "Colin, head out and eyes on that team. Javier, check the room. Luke, move your ass."

Luke unsheathed a knife, cut the man from the chair, and hauled him to his feet. "That lady isn't anything compared to me, asshole."

"You want money, I've—"

Luke shook him silent and kept him in hand as they left and bounded down the stairs, moving to a waiting Expedition. Luke was the last one in after he threw their mark in the backseat. Ryder was behind the steering wheel.

They pulled out, passing the woman, who was leaning against the side panel of a black Lotus. There had to be two hundred yards between them, and her anger was still palpable. With dark hair, full lips, and a body made for sex, she was clothed in a dress that left nothing to the imagination. Yet somehow, despite the surroundings and where he'd just seen her, she was the classiest, most exotic thing he'd ever seen.

"Fuck," he grumbled. She was like his fantasy come true—looking like that, leaning against a high-performance sports car, ready to slit a trafficker's throat. His hard-on was back. "Who the hell *is* she?"

They tore through a neighborhood that should have scared her, should've made *anyone* uncomfortable with the crime and poverty. He'd read through Mercier's corporate front of a website and every file he could get on the daughter of the trafficking kingpin, so he knew on paper what they wanted the world to know. Brilliant, beautiful, and business-minded. Nothing he'd learned was anything like what he saw. She was straight-up badass, dressed in couture, hell-bent on an unknown mission.

Felipe shook his head. "She's a means to an end."

Luke turned quickly, ready to pounce, but Colin put a hand on his shoulder, changing his attack to merely a question about the obvious. "Are you stupid?"

Rivera sneered. "Do I look stupid?"

"That and so much more."

Felipe was likely one of the sons of the man who'd sold Luke's girlfriend. The intel from Delta's HQ had named the Riveras without a doubt.

He didn't *want* to know what happened to his girlfriend; he *had* to know. Felipe would give him details on the past while the taskforce learned useful intel. Intelligence was the purpose of this job, wasn't it?

He glanced at Cade, who was patched in to their headquarters, having a conversation about Madeleine Mercier. Luke found his attention riveted to Cade, and he was hungry to hear about her—*no*. He pinched his eyes shut. She was the enemy.

Damn it.

"Thanks, Parker," Cade said to HQ and gave Luke a scowl. Whatever had come from Parker, Delta's IT guru, wasn't going to be great.

"What?" Luke asked.

The guy shook his head. "Shit, brother."

"What?"

"We now know a lot more about your girl."

Your girl. She wasn't his girl. Definitely wasn't anyone else's girl. But she was his present-for-the-last-few-weeks thought.

"Lady in the dress?" Luke asked. Cade couldn't mean any other girl—except his girlfriend from long ago—but no details were left for Delta to dig up on her.

Cade's harsh features mocked him. "Yeah. I'm talking about the lady in the dress. Mercier management."

Felipe twitched and shifted and twitched again. "She's the spawn of Satan."

Great. Terrific. A peanut gallery. He turned back to Cade. "Lady in the dress. What's the deal?"

His face drew tight. "She's Mercier's only living heir."

"Which we knew," he snapped back.

"She's been groomed from day one to take over the empire. Has her hands in everything. The girls. The drugs. The life. *Everything.* Brother, she is bad news, of the bad-seed variety. It's in her blood."

* * * *

Three days had passed since the incident at Hotel Miranda. With a cup of Cuban coffee resting between her fingers, Maddy stared at the security-camera feed from outside their offices, looking at the man she had run into twice in less-than-normal circumstances. *What is Luke doing here?* She should be terrified even though, through the live grayscale image, his eyes breathed fire and his lips offered a promise she couldn't quite define.

Knock.

Maddy pushed the tiny cup and saucer away, knowing she didn't need the jolt of caffeine, and waited for her assistant to enter.

"Ms. Mercier?" Kylie hadn't let him in, rightfully so. She didn't let anyone into their secure offices unless they were cleared on the roster. Love had impossibly high security measures, which gave her high-def visuals of the man wanting in.

Maddy couldn't look away from the screen, nor could she think clearly. He was attractive, but attraction was boring. Pretty people were her job, and looks could be bought, especially in Miami. But that man—with all his glaring, angry glory—had passion. That was an interesting quality. He also knew far more about her than she did him.

Taking an uneasy breath, she nodded. "Let him in."

"What...?"

Never had Kylie questioned her, so repeating herself was abnormal. "I said open the door. Tell him where to find me."

Kylie demurred, realizing that questioning a direct order was a very bad idea, but Maddy let it go. The DEA man had her full attention.

Less than a minute later, the door to Maddy's executive office flew open. It bounced against the wall, and there he stood. Over six feet of solid muscle ignored Kylie, who trailed behind him, and centered his attention on Maddy.

"We're good, thank you." With a nod to a slack-mouthed Kylie, Maddy turned to the raging man. "Nice to see you again. No handcuffs?"

Luke's expression tightened. "No."

However, the look in his eye... Something was going to happen.

"Would you like to have a seat?"

His intense stare didn't waver, and her sarcasm didn't throw him off. Men didn't get to her. *No one* got to her. But the fluttering of her stomach and heart was altogether new. It was an uncertain feeling.

"No," he growled and stalked across the expansive space to Maddy, making her pulse race.

A knot she wasn't familiar with formed in her throat, and taking a deep breath, Maddy felt anticipation—of what, she didn't know—race through her veins. "Then what do you want?"

"I need to know something."

The rumble of his words made her skin flush. At just his timbre, heat bloomed deep within her, catching her off guard. Flutters that she couldn't describe and didn't want to stop.

Needing to escape her internal unknown, she headed for her desk where she could hide from afar and assess everything from her reaction to her unfamiliar thoughts. "What do you *need to know?*"

His strong fingers grabbed her shoulder, swung her to face him, and made her skin sizzle under his hold. Swallowing an unsteady gasp, she shivered as his hand flexed into her flesh. "You climbed out a window and scaled a building."

She pulled her composure back together. Luke was here to investigate her, which made more sense than him letting her leave Rivera's side. She didn't need to be anywhere near this man. Unexpected behavior and a badge were a lethal combination. "The woman who let you in can give you my attorney's phone number. Feel free to make an appointment." Even though asking him to leave almost hurt.

His dark eyes narrowed as he let go of her shoulder. "Beautiful, if I wanted to have that type of conversation with you, I'd yank your sweet ass in."

Her eyes went wide. People didn't surprise her, but between his *beautiful* and the flashes of warmth blossoming inside her, she struggled to maintain her composure. "Then what is it you want?"

He smiled, a simple, handsome, perfect grin. It was almost sweet, definitely sexy, and it hit her like a tidal wave, stronger than downing a dozen Café Cubanos, as did the realization that the absurd and addictive flush tinging her body was arousal.

"I'm curious," he said.

"About?" All she could concentrate on was whether or not he excited her.

"Who climbs balconies for a helicopter airlift?"

When he stared as though impressed and disgusted simultaneously, she ignored a storm of internal questions. "I should've handled that differently."

"I don't care about your actions."

"You don't?" But he was law enforcement. She evaded him after being *caught.*

"How did you know to do that?" he pushed.

"I know a lot." Though she knew nothing about why she flushed or how his words could almost be felt against her skin.

"Madeleine Mercier." His face was harsh and handsome while her name sounded lyrical.

She memorized the edges of his face and the punch of his voice. Scars hid in his eyes. He had her beat when it came to pain and darkness. All of that made him even more attractive.

She was twenty-one years old and had never even been kissed—completely unbelievable if not for her family's business. Attraction seemed disgusting. Irresponsible. Revolting and sickening. The list went on and on. She had never experienced what she was feeling for Luke Brenner.

He wasn't on her father's payroll, nor was he hunting her. He was like…a hero. A savior. The idea made her shy away, both emotionally and physically.

His eyes narrowed again, assessing. Looks and reactions were her job. Knowing what people wanted, that was her livelihood. She was a master at reading what those in front of her couldn't find the words to say. But there she was, reacting without fear of consequence. All because he could somehow help her?

His mood darkened. "You're a traf—"

"Careful." Her lips flattened. If he said the wrong thing, she'd have to back away when, for the first time in her life, she was wondering how it might feel to have strong arms wrap around her, to feel protected in a way that Mercier or Hale couldn't offer.

He inched closer despite her warning. "Why should I be?"

"Words and actions change everything. What you've done and said, to this point, you can stay." She paused, thinking over the implications of what she'd agreed to but not caring. "You're not safe for me, but for some reason, I think you also…*are*."

"Why?" he asked, his voice huskier.

"You're a good person, aren't you?"

"Yeah, I am." He studied her for what seemed like years. "And you're not who everyone thinks you are."

"*Non*," she whispered, letting her French slide out. "No one knows me."

He stepped closer again. Mere inches separated them. "No one can make the connection to the trafficking. Mercier is that good.

Help me."

"Please don't talk about it."

He mumbled a curse. "They're infallible."

She took a ragged breath. "*No one* is infallible—" *Shoot.* She'd just announced her unhappiness in the Mercier ranks. Maddy pulled herself together again. "I own a modeling agency and sit on the corporate board of my family's company."

"Family company, my ass." Luke shook his head without dropping their eye contact. "You're part of the problem, or you're not." He reached for her elbow, and she expected him to grab her, to manhandle her until the truth poured from her lips, but his fingers grazed her forearm, stilling on her elbow. "What are you? Problem or not?"

She was *not.* Yet of course she was. "You have to leave."

"What is making you think so damn hard right now? Excuses? Lies?" His thumb rubbed the underside of her arm, making goose bumps tingle. "The truth, Ms. Mercier?"

The truth was she was a victim of her father, of circumstances, trying her hardest to make right with the only certainties she had known. No one could help her to the extent she needed. But the other truth was Luke was still touching her, and that topsy-turvy, warm feeling of arousal was attraction. An unfamiliar feeling that had never occurred before was happening with *her enemy.*

"Please remove your hand from me." Though she wanted anything but.

He stepped closer, letting their sides touch. This was what the fuss was, what made people stupid—the crushes, the cravings, the need, and the love. A shock of awareness moved through her stomach, deep to where she already wanted him, and it scared the hell out of her.

"Why would I?" He bent down and growled close to her ear. "Tell me a reason."

A thousand reasons and realities should have fallen off her tongue, yet none would come. Strands of her hair fell across her cheek, and his hot breath made them tickle her skin.

"You think you know so much." Her voice shook, almost a whimper. Something she needed but could never have stood before her, and if it never happened again for the rest of her life, she would miss the high.

Towering over her, he leaned in. "I do."

"You're wrong," she promised.

"Not often, beautiful. Traffickers ruined my belief in humanity. Are you a pretty face oblivious to your world, or are you what's wrong with it?"

Maddy jutted her chin up, unwilling to be either. "You don't know enough to wrap your head around what it is I do or why I do it."

He pulled back. "Tell me why you were with Felipe Rivera."

Finally, a simple question. "Because he lied about who he was. He hurt one of my girls. I *am* her protector. He took what he was not granted, and for that he will learn a hard reality of life."

"And that is?"

"I believe in revenge. I believe in payment. I believe in why I do what I must. There's no other way. I believe in her right to say yes or no. I believe more than you can fathom."

"Bullshit." His nearly black eyes shone. "You sell people. These models? Your fancy companies hiding behind international laws? All fake."

He'd crossed their line, but she didn't care. Her breaths came faster, and she needed him to understand at least one piece of her puzzle. "I wouldn't lie about Felipe Rivera."

He got into her face. "You would!"

Her pulse raced. "He hurt someone close to me, and this is one of the few times I *can hurt back*!"

"You're insane." He closed the distance between them, and his hips hit hers. "Messed up in the head."

"You have no idea," she breathed.

Luke moved them hard and fast. The back of her thighs hit her desk. His erection bulged in his pants. That should have made her want to vomit, but the repulsion wasn't there. Her eyes bulged at her own enjoyment, and as his strong hands wrapped around her waist, lifting her onto the edge of her desk, she didn't fight him off.

If anything, she wanted it to happen again. "You don't know what you're doing to me," she whispered. "You wouldn't believe it if I told you. Please. Leave."

His impossibly perfect lips were mesmerizing, and he watched her mouth intently. They were in a standoff—righteous versus vulgar, and all she wanted was her first kiss.

"Try me," he said.

God... "I can't. You're law enforcement."

"Some days I am. Most days I'm not."

What did that mean? For hire? Like Hale? Or worse? "A mercenary?"

"I'm a hunter."

The hunter and the virgin. What a combination. "And I'm your prey."

His eyes closed as he stepped back, dragging his hands from her hips to her knees. Then, as strongly as he'd come in, he left.

Alone and aroused, Maddy hated what she wanted from him and couldn't wait until they clashed together again.

CHAPTER FIVE

Five hours into an interrogation not worth the time spent traveling to Miami, Luke kicked the door open and walked out of the room, which stank of sweat and lies. Today marked nine days since Rivera had been in custody, the sixth day since he'd come face to face with Maddy Mercier at her office, and he couldn't shake her from his head.

Rivera couldn't remember Luke's old girlfriend, and for that sin, the man could stay locked in place. The Delta-MacKenzie task force had turned him over to the local feds, but at least Cade granted Luke the ability to stay with Rivera until he learned something, anything, about what had happened years before. But the trafficker hadn't shared new intel—it wasn't going well.

Luke paced the length of the dank hallway. *Enough for today.* His gut burned. These were the jobs he existed for—finding the perpetrators and destroying their factions, then rescuing the girls and cleaning up narcotics. The buzz of his cell phone stole his attention back to his dark reality. Luke unholstered it. *Cade.* "Yeah, boss."

"Get what you need?"

"No."

"*Can* you get what you need?"

Translation: Was Luke searching for a forgotten memory, a passing thought from too long ago? "I'll get what I need. Got decent details on the Rivera and Mercier cartels."

"He knows more than he's given up?"

"Yeah." Luke nodded, rubbing a hand over his eyes, kneading the bridge of his nose, finally noticing the soreness of his knuckles from his last fight. At least he had that slight bite of pain to feed off of. He needed it, especially after—his mind jumped back to Maddy. He hadn't touched her in the way he wanted to...but when he left, his heart had run away, his muscles tense and needing more of her.

"Luke—"

He shook his head, pulling himself back. "Yeah, boss."

"What do you think?"

"Yeah, man. I..." *Shit.* "What did you say?"

"Get your head in the game."

"It is." Luke tamped the rage running close beneath his skin. "Now, what did you say?"

"She had the same thing in mind as you. Maybe not the same reason, not as deep. But same."

"She, who?"

"The Mercier woman. The one you went to scout. Jesus fuck, tell me it wasn't the wrong decision to let you follow up."

"It was the right one."

"What have you learned?"

"Not as much as I'd like." That was the truth. "What'd Delta learn about her?"

"She's retaliatory."

Luke grumbled. "She's a trafficker. That's what they do."

"Rivera worked over one of her models, and she was out for blood. We interrupted what, according to Parker's intel, could have been a very painful night for Felipe Rivera."

Revenge... But that didn't make her any better of a person. "Not sure what to think about that." He mulled over the vixen with the flashy ride who'd been as comfortable in the ghetto as she was in her office. Yet when he'd been turned on and pressing against her, she seemed as though she'd never been touched, the way her surprise shone through her bravado. That made him even more curious.

"Believe it," Cade said. "She has a reputation."

Luke's head pounded. A craving to feel something besides heartache and vengeance rushed through him. He needed to fight, whether it was with gunfire or his fists, as long as the pain was deep enough to leave a lasting mark.

"Damn," he growled. "I'm out. Feds can wrap this dude."

Luke ended the call. Cade wouldn't be pissed. Over the last few weeks, they'd found a balance between MacKenzie Security and Delta team jobs. Every person on the team knew how Luke survived, how he blew off steam without killing everyone in the room. He could find a fight in any city, at any op location. Barroom brawl. Street fight. Underground ring. This was Miami—big city, lots of money, lots of sins. With his mouth watering for pain and adrenaline coating his mindset, Luke needed to get outside and into trouble.

* * * *

The crowd hummed. Bodies packed against bodies, swaying and cursing. The amber light in the far corners of the warehouse tinted every face orange, no matter their skin color. Murmurs and chants for blood started to rumble. Luke's eyes were closed, and bass thumped in his ears. His head nodded to the beat, and he embraced the current of excitement running through the room.

"Ready!" a man shouted into a bullhorn.

The warehouse exploded with a dull thunder. The shouted vibrations and anticipatory murmurs flowed through the crowd, shoulder to shoulder, standing room only.

"Fighters, front and center."

Luke's eyes opened as he locked on his man. *Puerto Rican lookin'*. He was just as tall as Luke, though wider. The scars on his face and the fight in his dark eyes promised Luke a well-matched fight. Luke would have to pull from his depths to win, to feel the pain he craved and still come out on top.

"In the red…" the bullhorn man crowed into the ready room, but his words faded into the rumbling.

His opponent bounced on his toes, flanked by two men. One slapped his face, the other rubbing his muscles. That was what they did—the entourage banking on their winnings.

Too bad.

"And new to us, the white-boy fighter who goes simply by Luke."

The crowd booed and jeered. Luke had no one in his corner. He didn't want it, and he always ensured Delta was never there—no show of sportsmanship, no moral support. Because this was about one thing, getting his fix. Feeling better. Numbing the outside world. He'd draw out the fight for as long as he needed, then his internal monitor would give the go-ahead, and Luke would shut it down, take his win, own his pain. And he'd disappear into the shadows a little calmer, ready to survive the world for another bit.

It was addiction, pure and simple. His mouth watered with the proximity to what he needed. There was nothing honorable about why he fought. Brock and Cade both knew what they needed to know, and that was that. Only his teammate Javier seemed to really understand.

"Fight!"

Like the world fading away, the cursing, smoking, shouting crowd melted into a blur that surrounded him. The people became white noise. Luke focused on the fight in front of him.

The man came fast. He cut right, left. Sharp, biting punches that Luke took. On purpose. Pain exploded, and *God*, it was like heaven. His opponent hadn't expected the easy shot, didn't understand why Luke had all but leaned into his fists. The only things he'd avoid were head shots.

The white noise burst, evidently stoked at the possibility of their local, reigning champ winning so easily, but also at the sound of the impact, flesh colliding with flesh. The dull thumps, the grunts, the trickles of sweat flying through the air accelerated these people.

Luke threw a jab. Took a cheap shot because he wanted to embrace the sting, savoring the pain. His blood flowed, and his mind cleared. He could breathe. Moving back, he rolled his shoulders and listened to the crowd boo for his knockout.

Too bad for the fighter opposite Luke—he had his high, the delicious bloodlust-soaked burst of sanity that made him tick. Luke morphed into another man. He wanted more than to accept the pain. He needed to give it. His fists flew. His body jabbed, evaded, ducked, and spun.

The white noise roared. His opponent stumbled, caught off guard. Stance correct and reassessing Luke, the man recalibrated and swung forward.

But Luke was done, having taken and given as much as he needed. He didn't want one moment more. A swift, vicious one-two punch flew, perfectly choreographed, from his fists, and the local champion flew back, back arching, eyes shut. He landed with a bounce, and the bodies surrounding them pinched closer, screaming their disapproval, demanding a rematch, hollering for the downed man to rebound.

Luke shook out his fists. No gloating was needed, no body guys to tend to his bleeding wounds or to wash out his mouth. No. He rolled his shoulders again and turned. Done.

Finally, he was able to take a breath, as he hadn't been able to in weeks. This moment was a calm to his storm. He pushed into the crowd as his lungs slowed and sweat poured. It dripped into his eyes, and he savored that burn, the same as he did with his bruises and brokenness.

The crowd parted as he pushed, his gaze effortlessly sweeping the room as a renewed spirit took over him—until the warm, comforting high froze. He saw her.

Her.

The woman registered in his mind, and she was standing just feet in front of him. A couple inches shorter than he, even in heels, and in a bright and vibrant dress that stood out in the dank room, she radiated energy that he couldn't explain. It was sex. It was power. The confidence and confusion were intermixed. The effect slapped him harder than any hit he'd just taken. He stepped closer but stayed silent.

"Luke Brenner." His name on her tongue, soft and quiet in the harsh sound chamber, was magic. A salve. A soothing touch that cooled him as much as it heated him in a very different way from the fire of exertion or the pain of injury. And he hated it. Hated her. Just as much as he wanted it. Everything he stood against, she somehow was everything he'd ever wanted to touch, to kiss—the softness that must be her. But with their eyes locked, he knew that softness was equally opposed by whatever angst and deceit was locked inside her.

So very much like him.

His feet moved forward, his mind almost an unwilling

participant. But he said nothing, watching the sensual curve of her lips and wondering if his addiction to pain had changed into desire for a woman he wanted but would never touch. He wished they were alone again, but he didn't acknowledge her, the enemy—his prey, as she'd so aptly put it.

Instead, he stepped to the side, but her hand gripped his sweat-soaked bicep, nails squeezing into flesh. That slowed him, slowed his world.

"Get off, Maddy."

Her nails bit into his skin, and the intense satisfaction at the tiny pinches was dangerous. "You're on my turf."

"Right. So was I the other day. Then you were shaking like a leaf. Now you're hanging on me to stay." That facet of her didn't make sense either. "You stalked me? Tracked me?" However, that didn't make sense. He hadn't been followed, hadn't had a tail.

The corners of her mouth quirked up. "This is my world. These are my fights. You think you know Mercier, but you have no idea about me."

With that, she let go of his bicep, then turned. The crowd parted to her, an obvious sign of respect. They knew her, moved for her, gave her room, not just standing shoulder to shoulder. And as his gaze followed theirs, it became clear they feared her.

"What don't you own?" he shouted after her. "The girls. The models. The fighters. Your fancy cars."

Slowly, she glanced over her shoulder. "Come and find out."

CHAPTER SIX

Maddy controlled every detail in her life—who worked for her, how they behaved, what they said, and what they did. She helped the girls. She gained traction in her father's world. *Everything* was controlled. Until she'd met the man following her.

His footsteps trailed away, and her ears ached to hear him in the crowd. His fast breaths, that sculpted, inked chest rising and falling, and his powerful legs swishing in the mesh shorts hanging low on his hips were almost all she could think about. When she'd heard they had a new fighter asking for the best on the streets, her curiosity was piqued. But when she saw him, the same physical and mental reactions as before nearly brought her to her knees.

Her confident stride was a farce as she shook inside. *Her* chest rose and fell as quickly as his. Maddy was more turned on and distracted than the last time they'd been together.

They abandoned the crowded warehouse, still without another word exchanged. The power pulsed in the air. Luke wasn't a follower. He had dominated her in Love's office before, which she replayed over and over, deciding that fight for control of the conversation was intense *and* enjoyable.

Sex was business. Attraction was effortlessly decipherable, and domination was an easy sell, but this was personal. She looked over her shoulder, watching him stalk and scowl. Her Lotus waited outside the warehouse doors. The night was warm as she threw them open, but it was still cooler than inside, and the air wasn't sweaty and musky. It was almost sweet.

She slowed even as she knew he wouldn't. Behind her, his hard-muscled, sweat-slicked body pressed her against the car. Simply reacting, her back arched against him as he covered her. Maddy swayed, letting the cool window glass tease her hypersensitive skin.

Hot breath burned through the hair against her neck. "I don't play games."

"I do, so we have a problem." Her eyes closed and her belly tightened when his teeth scraped her skin. She was getting herself into a situation she wouldn't know how to handle. Of course she was playing games. She was pretending to be who he thought she was.

"Get over yourself, beautiful."

His attitude did bad things for her, and Maddy moaned as his teeth repeated the sensual scrape.

Luke spun her and pressed her back against the car. "Your fights?"

Breathless, she nodded. "I was told a new fighter started asking around. He wanted the best, the worst, all rolled into one. *That*, I have." She'd put her best against Luke and watched her fighter go down in the bare-knuckle bout.

Maddy knew pain.

She knew torment.

She'd never known a man wrecked with both more completely than this one.

They were made from the same fabric even if they were in different sexual universes. Something had happened to him that made him want to hurt. Somewhere along life's ugly path, he'd been destroyed, only to come back invincible. And knowing all that, she embraced her short, choppy breaths and encompassing arousal.

"Give me your keys," he growled quietly. The wave of his words swam over her, amplifying her want.

She swallowed, drunk on the moment. "No."

He pressed his hips to hers, flexing his thick erection between them. His masculine scent and sweat-dampened hair intoxicated her. She was almost ashamed.

"Keys, woman."

Her eyes sliced to challenge him, hoping another *no* would

bring more of his weight against her. She shook her head.

"Now."

"Why?" Her bottom lip hung open. She could almost taste his skin on her tongue. Could almost feel his kiss when she'd never had that type of touch before—fascinating and terrifying.

Another hard hip flex. "I'm not doing you here."

"Didn't ask you to." Though she would have to run from sex against a car as her first time, even if she couldn't keep her hands off him, because it would hurt. Guilt flooded her, that she hadn't been able to save more girls. The wicked wants of arousal disappeared, freezing in place despite Luke surrounding her.

He growled. "A trafficker who plays hard to get? Hot and cold?"

"Call me what you want." She tilted away from him. "I'm the only chance to change that."

"Change what?" Disbelief brooded angrily in his black eyes.

"You don't know what or why things happen. Certainly not in my world."

He scoffed, but he didn't back away as a glint flashed in his eyes. His jaw's hard line was inches from her face. His throat bobbed. The tattoos on his skin were scorched into her memory. Angels and demons. Tribal designs and beautiful words. Some scripts swirled while others were blocked and blacked, harshly contrasting the ornate ones.

"You and I. We're one and the same," she whispered.

His dark eyebrows bit together. "What is it that you think you see?"

"Everything." The pain. The distrust. The hunt for something out of reach.

"No." He shook his head. "I hate that I want to fuck you, fuck evil. We are *nothing* the same."

Her right hand swung to slap his face. He caught it, his strong hand wrapping around her wrist. His grip flexed, and electricity mixed with the discomfort, shooting all the way to her spine. Her left hand swung for him. His grip met that one, too.

"You're looking for a fight?" he asked incredulously.

Wrists in his grip, she had no idea what she was doing. Her head spun, reason and reality slipping away. "I don't know."

He backed an inch. "What's with that?"

"What?"

"The out-of-nowhere quiet response."

She shrugged, hating that he saw something vulnerable that she never should have shown.

His lips turned into a wary grin. "There's more than one side to you."

"I already told you that."

"Give me your keys."

Somehow, when Luke saw her defenseless side, it was a mental go-ahead to leave with him, *driving*. "They're in the ignition."

His brows went up. "Trusting, are we?"

"In this neighborhood?"

He nodded.

"More than trusting."

As his mind worked that over, Luke wrapped his hands around her, lifted her as if she were air, and seconds later, planted her in the passenger seat.

"This is all about sex?" he asked.

Her eyes jumped to his. "Yes." *Right?* Because if a sexual urge existed once in her life, she should move forward. Even if her nerves were flooding in a way she'd never experienced *and* her mind was making calculated mistakes.

* * * *

Dropping the super sports car into gear, Luke could have blamed his heavy erection on the horsepower under his control. But that wasn't it. The woman he couldn't keep his mind from had her soulful eyes on him, and her skirt drifted up as she repositioned in her seat. She was soft, too soft for the world she seemed content to carouse in, and her delicate fingers slid on her legs like in some subconscious boudoir striptease.

"Nice ride," he said.

"Thanks. It's just a car, though. I didn't pick it. But it fits the part."

"If you picked your own ride?"

"What would it be?"

He nodded, more curious than he should've been.

Her eyes closed, and she leaned back, humming to herself as though she'd never wondered exactly what kind of car she would want. "Oh!" She smiled then tried to hide it. "A convertible. A silver one."

"Make or model?"

"Doesn't matter. So long as the top goes down."

Interesting. Her semi-hidden smile bloomed from sweet to sinful. "What about you?"

"I have a truck."

"No name or model," she teased.

"You've got jokes." Luke watched her out the corner of his eye, caught off guard by this very normal side of her, sweet, almost flirting in a shy way—not the aggressive, in-control woman in the middle of an underground fight club.

"I guess maybe I do."

"You guess?"

"Yes, I guess."

"Like you're trying to figure out the world or something, huh, beautiful?"

"Seems like that's my new favorite thing. *Oui.*"

That made his lips twitch, a hint of a smile, and he couldn't remember the last time that had happened. Luke turned a corner, having no idea where to go.

"Mira House Hotel."

He knew where that was and dropped the gear, surging through traffic toward a hotel that was only blocks away.

Music played from top-of-the-line speakers, and they stayed silent until he pulled into the hotel's driveway. "You live here?"

"I have a penthouse suite on standby."

A swanky hotel room waited for her? His eyes cut to hers. "Do this often?"

She laughed, quickly tamping down her reaction. "Never."

"Right." What to believe and what to call her on was always a question.

Bellhops stood by their doors, and as if on cue, her door was opened, as was his, and she was greeted by name. "Ms. Mercier, good evening. Will anyone else from Love join us tonight?"

Love… Ironic. Nothing about someone like Maddy could love. She was depraved. Yet he was following her, ready to take her body the second he could.

Leaving the Lotus, Luke powered around the hood, catching glimpses from people nearby. He was still bare chested, with a bruise swelling one cheek. He walked past the moneyed guests, watching them stare at his tattoos and mesh shorts. On his face, they surely saw the demons of a lust-fueled, angry man. A dangerous predator. No one saw the trafficker who pimped women as she stood awaiting him.

Luke stopped and towered above her. "Your company, Love. Is it real?"

"Most things *are* actually what they seem. Unless you're not looking correctly."

"Playing games again," he mumbled.

"Then again, there are apparently shades of real, of right and wrong. The DEA agent and the trafficker, as you keep reminding me, heading to the penthouse?"

"I'm not on DEA's payroll."

"That's right. You're a hunter."

The way she said it made him want to grin, as though she didn't feel endangered, and he knew she shouldn't. Luke wanted more from her than an arrest, and that was clouding his judgment and blurring his goal. "Let's go."

She nodded, and he fell in step beside her. They passed the concierge, who subtly nodded to her as they headed to the elevators. Everyone knew her. He missed nothing, not the looks and glances, but he couldn't read minds, and his interest was stoked.

An elevator arrived immediately, and still in silence, they boarded. She took out a card and scanned it, then hit the P button. He turned, curious about how she had everything from the suite to the attention of all who worked there. "Do you own the hotel?"

"No." Again, she gave a careful smile.

"There's a first."

The corners of her mouth twitched, broadening her grin.

The elevator opened into a gorgeous hallway that ended at one door.

"It's open," she said.

He tried the handle, and the door opened easily. "You keep yourself a room on the ready, unlocked. Trusting..."

"Pays to have a place you can go without question."

"No one is paying you tonight, beautiful." He took in the opulence. *Holy shit.* The suite had to be packed with a hundred thousand dollars' worth of furnishing.

"Not every transaction is about money."

"Yes—"

"There's beauty..." Her gaze fell across his chest. "There's pleasure. There are new experiences."

They walked into the bedroom, not touching, still flirting, and he needed to run away from her but couldn't. "A dirty game of cops and robbers."

She opened her mouth to speak but instead nodded.

Everything inside him burned hot. His chest was tight, and his muscles ached.

A hunger, a curiosity, and a shyness surfaced when he least expected it, making him want to stroke her cheek, to ask her questions to figure out their undeniable draw. "Why do you trust me, Maddy?"

She blinked. "I have no idea."

"You said you were my prey. What do you want? To hurt? Be saved? What is this?" Because whatever it was, it was addictive. He was running on a high that he couldn't explain.

"I'm a businesswoman, except that I've been put into a world that I hate. *I have to survive.* I didn't have the luxury of growing up with crushes and loves. For the first time, I see the possibility of something that changes me, and I *want*—deeply, badly, terribly—I *want* someone to...make me."

"Make you what?"

A challenge broadcasted on her face as she lifted her chin. "Make me feel."

Needing to feel? That was his problem, his need—to feel pain to feel better. "You want what?"

"Just..."

"What, Maddy? Say it."

"I don't know! Maybe I'm as screwed up as—" She pinched her eyes, shaking her hair as she stepped close to the bed.

"Dominate me. Make me feel it. You. This. Us."

His eyes narrowed, assessing her request. It was almost as though she didn't know what else to ask for, what else to like. But coming from her world, domination was probably what she knew. She wanted to feel, she was asking for it the way she'd experienced, and fuck it all, but there was something about her that he couldn't say no to. It wasn't the sex. He had no idea what it was, just that vibe that there was more. "That's what you want, beautiful?"

"I need it."

But what did he need? To avenge the past. His mind raced back to their first interaction, when she stood near a bed, positioned in an eerily similar way, while other women sat on the mattress. His throat closed as he reviewed what he knew then and now. "Where was the other girl?"

"Excuse me?" Her face blanched.

"On the balcony-climbing day, Maddy. Intel said there was another girl."

"No." Her cheeks pinked, and her mouth stayed parted as though she had so much more to say.

"Where is she? What did you do for her?" Suddenly, Luke had a glimmer of hope that Maddy Mercier wasn't the devil. "I don't want your secrets. Your resources. But I need to know. What happened to her?"

Seconds ticked. "I bought her."

"What does that mean?"

"To save her."

Not the devil. His soul sighed as a hot rush ran through him. Cade had said she was bloodthirsty, but Luke couldn't stay away and couldn't believe he was this drawn to depravity. That second, they had a connection—the same target, the same goal. What buzzed between them was more than sexual. It was primal. If Maddy wanted to lose control with him, he'd take it. If she was able to rescue a girl, he'd respect it. Their minds had melded. He'd never met a woman who mirrored him. He'd never met *anyone* who mirrored his demons.

CHAPTER SEVEN

Power and dominance emanated from the chiseled man standing before Maddy. His presence electrified the air and slid over her skin, pulling down her dress and teasing her core. All of this he did without so much as a physical touch. But she was way, *way* in over her head. Never having been kissed, she'd just told a man like Luke to dominate her.

Losing her virginity was going to be awful. But that was her destiny. She sold sex and didn't know the first thing about it—only how she'd grown up and what she'd been taught. That was to submit, to be trained. Nothing about how she felt on the inside and what she wanted.

Nerves getting the best of her, she wavered but didn't let him see her fearful excitement. Luke turned, and the visual display of color deeply inked on his skin was beautiful. His back muscles were taut, his shoulders sharp, and the column of his spine trailed into the gym shorts he'd fought in. They covered the well-defined curves of his ass, and she wanted to touch, to really feel the power tied in him.

When he twisted back to her, an erotic storm was playing on his face. His pupils dilated, his skin flushed. "Dress off, beautiful, and get on the bed."

Trembling, she stepped out of a shoe.

"Woman." He caught her startled gaze hard, which made her shiver. "I said *dress.*"

This was what she had asked for. Maddy stared at the slingback and slipped it back on, then unzipped the dress. With a simple shrug of her shoulders, the expensive fabric fell away, leaving her in lingerie and heels.

Luke sucked a quiet breath, his eyes drinking her in. As hard and harsh as he was, the savoring appreciation filled her with something in addition to lustful need.

With a nod, she moved to the bed and crawled on, never letting his gaze go.

"On your back."

She did, tilting her head to keep her focus on him. Luke crossed his thick arms, making his biceps bulge and his forearms flex. His shoulders were broad, and his erection hung heavy in the shorts, which hid nothing.

"Spread your legs for me."

Her stomach jumped, and her heart stopped, but she did as directed.

He stalked closer to the bed. "Hands above your head, beautiful."

Again, she did as told. Shivers cascaded over her as he took long strides toward her. He leaned on the edge of the bed, and her nipples were surprisingly hard, and the mound between her legs was hot. An aching neediness coiled deep below her stomach, and she thought if she could hold on to this feeling, she'd be set for a lifetime of daydreams.

"Do not move." He brought his angry face to hers, with just inches between their lips. His chest didn't touch her chest, and their arms didn't glance off one another.

All she wanted to do was feel his skin, but he didn't give her that gift.

"Not one inch." As quickly as he had hovered over her, Luke turned, headed to the bathroom, and shut the door.

What? Tempted to sit up, she closed her eyes and replayed the deep, shaking anger that she could feel he shared and decided *that* was the kind of energy she wanted deep inside her. Maddy didn't move.

The water turned on, and a realization hit. He was showering. Instantaneously, her mouth watered, and her ears burned. The sounds of him washing, naked and dripping, filled her thoughts.

Her breasts ached for his onslaught as much as her lips wanted to be kissed. Maddy was primed in a way that she didn't know existed, waiting and wanting. She *needed* him, and that blew her mind, having never *needed*...ever.

Anticipation crackled when the water shut off, and her core clenched, another amazingly new feeling. Seconds turned into years. The door cracked open, and steam and the scent of soap rolled in. Then there he was, towel around his waist, barefoot and focused on her.

The room warmed as steam wafted into the suite. The bedroom was luxurious. The trappings of the Miami penthouse were decadent. Yet the heat burning in Luke's eyes was the only thing worth looking at. How many hours had he spent sculpting his body to sheer perfection? How many hours had he spent under a tattoo artist's gun?

Her lips trembled as he towered over her, the shower's damp warmth making her react with a cascade of shivers. She bit her lip. "What are you going to do?"

"Dominate you, beautiful," he rasped. "Make you feel more than you ever have before. Just like you asked."

Her eyes shut as they rolled back, and the grit and scratch of his words ran over her senses. His hands hovered over her skin without making contact, heat radiating from his palms. She imagined how rough they were, maybe calloused, definitely strong. She recalled the possessive hold he had on her, how his long fingers demanded that she behave in her office, her domain.

Luke leaned his handsome face close. He smelled like soap, like clean, virile man. His lips were a dark pink, the hint of dark stubble scratching her cheeks. Without kissing her, his lips hovered close, floating across her cheek and toward her neck. Goose bumps erupted under the trail of almost-not-quite kisses, but neither his hands nor his mouth made contact.

Maddy shifted, unconsciously lifting her hips, arching her back the tiniest of degrees. A moan purred from her mouth, encompassing every deep, dark desire this man was eliciting from her. A fraction of air separated them. Electricity pulsed in her blood, strumming between her legs. "Please."

He pulled back enough that she knew a lash of his tongue

wouldn't happen, nor would she receive a bite of his teeth.

"You're teasing me."

Amusement danced on his face. His erection jutted from under the towel that hung dangerously low around his waist. If only it would fall. If only she could have his rigid length against her.

The tips of his fingers touched her hard nipples. His touch ran an almost nonexistent circle around the tight, lace-covered buds.

"God…" The sensation was astonishing. Her breathing hitched as his fingers drew their path more firmly. The back of his knuckles dragged from one peak to the next, and she found it ironic how the angriest, toughest man she'd ever come across was teasing her with pressure lighter than a breath.

"Why do you do what you do?" he asked as his hand began to explore her stomach, stroking from her breast to the top of her lacy thong.

With the models? She sucked a breath as his finger dipped into her belly button on the way back up. "Beautiful people make beautiful pictures."

"Liar." Down his hand went again. "That's not why, and I wasn't talking about Love."

Her eyes narrowed razor-sharp. "Not what we're here to talk—"

"Beautiful." Luke traced the top of the lace band again before following it to her hip and then drifting down that sensitive line where her leg met her mound. He didn't go past the fabric, didn't dip under the lace to the skin that was nearly crying for his touch. Just the simple torture he seemed so keen to dole. "I know the cartels, and I know Mercier." Over her thong-covered clit, he flicked his thumb slowly, making her writhe at the unexpected sensation. "And you aren't what you seem."

Panting, she shook her head. "You don't know as much as you think you do."

"I know there's a woman hard and cold as she is fragile and hot, lying before me, begging me to take away her ability to say no, her control, her attitude. I know—"

"I'm not fragile," she hissed, but for the first time in her life, she was…*hot*. Every time she thought she couldn't feel more explosive, he ramped her up again.

He laughed quietly as though he could read the desperation in her soul. "You're something." He bent, still not kissing her, but she could feel the heat from his lips hovering over her hip bone. "What do you like?"

Her eyes sank shut again, out of her control. "*That.*"

"Specific, baby."

"I don't know. Please."

His hands trailed up her thighs. "You want me here?"

She nodded, nearly moaning. "Yes."

His hands skipped to her stomach, smoothing over her breast. "Or here?"

"There too." Her skin was on fire, needling her to the point of insanity.

His black eyes burned into her skin. The look smoldered as much as it scared her. "Fuck, you're gorgeous. You wanna take my cock, you're gonna learn it's the best you've ever had."

His lips hit her neck, making her gasp, making her insane. She lost her mind, lost her censor. "It'll be the only I've ever had."

He froze and inched over her face. All of the emotion that had heated his cheeks and fired his gaze went flat. "*What?*"

"I…"

His face twisted. "What kind of game is that?"

"Uh, never mind. I—I don't know—"

"I'm not one of your sickos wanting a fucking virgin. I am *not* your clients." He pushed away. "I can't believe this."

She sat up, embarrassed and angry at who she was. "It's not what you think."

"Un-fucking-believable. I don't need this crap." Luke turned from her coldly and grabbed his shorts, stepping into them and complaining about the evils of traffickers before he left her alone on the bed.

Devastated, she twisted to watch him walk out. Words to stop him wouldn't come as unfurling desolation twisted her into the fetal position. Hot tears slid over her cheeks, the first time she'd cried over how screwed up she was.

* * * *

Luke's heart slammed in his chest as he reached the elevator. *A virgin? Bullshit.* That was the biggest load of crap. He punched the button and wanted to cling to the wall for fear he'd run back to Maddy's suite, strip her thong, and fuck her until they both came, screaming to the heavens that nothing could be better. Because she was a liar.

What the hell was his problem? She was the very definition of what he despised, and he'd almost…almost done everything she asked for because he couldn't say no. She held a power over him like nothing he'd ever experienced. He hated her for the attraction as much as for her past. Never had cock before? Bullshit! What level of screwed up was she?

The elevator chimed, and as he jumped in, his mind raced to the team. Cade knew he'd gone out to get his fighting fix, but if he heard Luke left with her, that'd be problematic.

Still bare chested and looking like he did—angry, dangerous, and horny as all hell—he earned his fair share of second glances from hotel guests. Surely someone was going to send security up to the penthouse to make sure Maddy was still kicking. He laughed. It'd take quite the man to fuck up that woman. She was ice cold, a total lunatic. A stabbing sensation hit his chest—*if someone did hurt her, or if she hadn't been lying…* He shook his head. If someone hurt her, one fewer trafficker would exist. That was his goal in life, so what did he care if this one was a pretty face who had never been touched?

Her words haunted his memory. What was her promise—she wasn't like what she seemed? That she had more than a surface-level need to retaliate. Who bought women only to save them? No one. Except Madeleine Mercier.

Luke ran his hands over his face as he exited the hotel. He had miles to his crash pad, and rolling his shoulders once, he took off at a run. He'd push himself again, hoping to feel a burn in his muscles, and maybe that ache would draw out the sweet sound of her voice trying to explain how she'd never been with a man before.

CHAPTER EIGHT

The Mercier office did not possess the same swank feel as Love. Maddy acted different here. Cold, more ruthless.

Hale loomed over what was basically a negotiation. His sidearm on his waist and his bulky arms crossed over his wide chest, he looked the part he was to play, the muscle. Sitting in front of her was Felipe Rivera's great uncle, a wealthy cartel man who wanted to throw money at the Mercier-Rivera problem. The man didn't want bad blood between their families, and he was making amends for Felipe, who had already been sprung from federal custody. But US federal agents were not Rivera's concern. He was concerned that she would exact her revenge against Felipe, which she would, and he wanted to make sure Papa was not irritated, which he was.

Maddy pursed her lips together. "Nothing, Mr. Rivera, that you've said changes my mind."

He'd gone from haughty to indignant to knowing. A thin sheen of sweat decorated his forehead. Miami's harsh heat wasn't making him perspire. The office was cool, almost to the point of cold. The uncertainty that danced in his eyes was an indication of fear. "We're all in business together."

"*We* are not."

"To some extent—"

"No, we are not."

"Ms. M—"

"I don't like *you*, and I despise your nephew. He was wrong to teach my father a lesson with my girl. For as much as this is business between our families, I want you gone."

He leaned back, a shimmer of relief working its way across his features. "I think we both know that I'm not going anywhere, and you don't have the clout to make that happen."

"We both know that your nephew will continue to be hunted."

His lips went flat again. "This conversation is a joke."

"He will go to jail for rape."

The uncle shook his head, as confident about his disagreement as her father was with his law-enforcement dealings. "The charges will never stick."

Maddy's molars ground. "I hope they don't. I hope Felipe roams the wild, waiting for the day that he"—she nodded toward Hale—"finds him."

Hale growled his interest and agreement.

"He's a barracuda." Maddy smiled. "Even meaner than he looks."

Rivera failed to hide a concerned glare. "What do you want?"

"He'll take a beating. But live. And you get out of South Florida. No more business with Mercier."

"He lives, and I get out of Miami."

"No."

His brow furrowed. "He lives, and we're out of business with Mercier."

Maddy smiled. "Deal."

"*He lives.*"

"Those are the terms. Now, leave."

This was not a man used to being bossed around. Bristling, he regained the composure that made him feared on the streets and stormed out.

Asshole.

Hale sauntered over, still glaring, but he fell into the chair that Rivera had been in. "Doing okay?"

"Of course," she snapped. But no, she was wound up more tightly than a cokehead in detox.

His all-knowing eyes narrowed, but he let it drop. "Schedule says you're scouting tonight."

"That's what it says, that's what I'm doing." Though after going one-on-one with the elder Rivera, she wanted to search for girls to save, not models who needed a sandwich. But she couldn't do the first one without the cover of the second, and truthfully, she did find enjoyment in that side of her business also. Dreams were made. Beautiful things were noticed—Maddy had made a point to find the models who weren't considered perfect by society standards. Then she kicked society's opinion on its ass when her models strutted their stuff. For what had once been awkward, with her light shining on it, was now hip. What had been considered a flaw was now a selling point.

She took a calming breath, trying to tap into the control that lassoed her anxiousness. "Yes, Hale. Tonight'll be good."

"You need to blow off some steam."

She smiled. The man knew her better than most. "True."

"Get yourself some fancy cocktail, do your thing, then try to relax."

Hale recognized everything that was Love and Mercier. They'd never been attracted to each other, nor had he given much advice on her plan to dismantle Mercier, but he was one of the only people who knew all about her virgin status, so where he might tell someone else to get laid, he would just tell her to relax.

"Maybe."

He cleared his throat.

"What?" she asked, feeling the intense gaze of a man determined to get answers.

"Know about that boy at Mira House."

Her tight smile pinched downward. "Whatever you think you know, nothing came of it." Her lips quirked. "Even if I wanted it."

"Interesting." He sat on the edge of her desk. "You two are cut from different cloth."

"Not at much as you would think."

"Heard he was at the fights."

Maddy smoothed her palms on her desk. "You heard a lot, Hale."

"I did." His handsome, scowling face tilted. "He drove the Lotus?"

Her eyes sank shut, and she breathed in deeply, remembering the power in Luke's command, the feel of the sports car under his control, and his body teasing hers at the penthouse. "Yes."

"Not sure he's good for you."

"Not sure I want good for me," she volleyed back.

"An asshole like that could hurt you in several ways."

Maddy tossed her head back, in her designer dress, surrounded by her perfect office, everything sexy and vibrant. "I *wanted* to find out what it was like. I felt something with him."

"Not like that. He's the authorities." He shook his head. "Careful. Always be careful. You've worked so hard on one thing. Don't suddenly find your mojo and mess it all up."

She didn't want to be careful, though. She wanted Luke, and the high from him would be enough to live off of if she never felt this way again. But Luke Brenner was gone. She knew it. The fighter-protector who brandished a gun as quickly as he threw his fists had disappeared from Miami and wanted nothing to do with her.

* * * *

The pop music beat vibrated in the VIP section. Expensive champagne chilled in buckets, and an entourage of staff surrounded her, but Maddy remained on edge. Her eyes roamed the crowd. A few faces slowed her search as her people brought talent by to introduce. Those ladies stayed, drinking bubbly and trying to figure out how best to finagle a spot as a Love model. God forbid anyone earn a spot because they were worth it, not because of what they could provide.

Maddy pinched her eyes shut and let the music's energy run through her. Ignoring the world, she sipped the champagne and prayed for it to take the edge off. She could find slight relaxation with a drink and a party, but that would not happen tonight. Her eyes sliced across the room, and in the sea of slamming, dancing svelte Miami bodies stood the reason why.

Luke. He was dressed to kill in a suit that confirmed the existence of a God who wanted women to swoon. Despite the atmosphere and the people surrounding her, she was unable to think clearly.

The music shifted suddenly, and Maddy broke the eye lock, uneasy about his presence and nervous about what he could want.

She turned toward the safe confines of her table. People wanted her attention, but Hale got what she communicated to him without even a word. He took off at her silent order to find Luke.

Minutes ticked by until he lumbered back, shaking his head. "Can't locate him."

"Good. Glad he's gone." But her insides twisted, and she wanted to know so much more about how he made her feel. "I'm headed out."

"Maddy." Hale stepped closer.

She brushed by him.

"Maddy," he growled.

Taking a deep breath, she pivoted. "Take the night off, Hale. The girls are covered. Kylie's got a bead on everyone I need names of from here. Forget I'm walking away."

"To him?"

Maddy nodded, unable to register how a commando look-alike could make a suit look better than when he wore his save-the-world gear. The scout in her wanted to stage a photo shoot with him. The woman in her didn't want another set of eyes on him.

"He's a bad one, Maddy."

"I know." A quick jab of her heart thumped in her chest. "But I can't stay away."

CHAPTER NINE

Neon lights colored the faces of the bodies milling on the sidewalks, lining up to get into bars and clubs. Most women were dressed in a few inches of fabric, but not the woman he had gone out to find. A black, skintight dress had hugged her luscious curves, and her dark hair hung onto her shoulders. The strands were silky soft, Luke knew from experience, but what he wouldn't do to thread his fingers through it...

Maddy Mercier was his newest form of pain, when he'd never known anything but violence could bring up the delicious feeling he craved. She was it, the newest drug of choice, similar to heroin—after one hit, the cravings were absurd, the withdrawals dangerous. She was like that. Maybe worse.

He powered down the street, watching the crowds lessen until the unmistakable *clack-clack* of stupid-expensive shoes followed him down a street where no sane woman would go. Luke spun slowly.

Across the club, there had been something about her that made the packed room fade away. But alone, on the street, with just her and him and this tension between them, their connection wasn't just one quality. It was everything from not trusting her, to hating her, to needing to taste her and take her more than he needed another brawl, another ops job, another *anything*. "You're following me."

"You're stalking me."

"Games are one thing." He took a step closer. "Lies are another."

"It wasn't a lie."

"Then a joke."

"I've never even been kissed."

"Damn," he growled, rubbing his temples. Confusion mixed with his irritation. At her. At himself. At the whole goddamn world. He hated who he was sometimes as much as he hated his history. "I can't deal with this. Get out of here. Go home. Go do whatever it is you do. Come up with crazy-ass stories and play your games."

"Trafficking is personal to you."

"No," he lied. "Not a sane person on earth supports that shit."

"What if the only way of life I've known is that?"

"Then you change it. You find cops, you tell someone. You walk away. You change it."

"I'm trying."

"You're a liar."

"You keep saying that, yet you're still here. Your eyes say you believe me, but your mouth doesn't agree."

"Beautiful…" He shook his head. "Yeah, it's personal."

"*Help* me."

His eyes widened. "Excuse me?"

"You're not on his payroll?"

"Your father?" He shrank back. "Hell no."

"You really are a hero, aren't you? Like a savior I never knew existed."

He took a step back, uncertain how she was baiting him. "No hero. I get shit done. That's it."

"Same. We're the same." Perfect skin and hungry eyes glared up as she stepped right to his chest. "You came to the club."

"Go home, princess."

"*Beautiful.*" Another inch disappeared between them. "I like it better when you call me beautiful."

His chest felt too tight, his hands too empty. "Don't tell me you're conceited too. Need to hear something nice? Go to the lackeys you pay. They'd gladly fawn over you."

"Trust me, they don't fawn."

"What do they do?"

She leaned into him, a truthful glint shining in her eyes. "Tell me the unvarnished truth."

His chest expanded, and his skin prickled, closing the distance. He couldn't tell if they were going to throw down in the street or fuck against the wall. He wanted both. The thick, rhythmic beats of his heart made blood pound in his neck. Wanting to squeeze her, to shake her, Luke moved one hand to her cheek, and she sighed. *Damn. Soft.* So soft, too fragile. All her venom was a front. He dragged his knuckles down to her jawline. His thumb brushed her bottom lip as her eyes went wide and her shallow breaths warmed the pad of his finger.

"You've never been with a man?"

"No."

"Liar." He closed the distance, in her face, feeling the heat of his words against the warmth of her lips. "You've never been kissed."

She shook her head. "Never."

His lips brushed hers, and she whimpered. One hand splayed against her back, and he pulled her closer with a harsh jerk, a stark contrast to the careful almost-kiss of their lips. His tongue darted out, testing her mouth. "Bet you taste sweet."

She swayed against him, her hips gently slipping side to side. "I don't know why, but I want more now that I've met you."

"Meaning?" he growled as his lips ran to her earlobe, and he kissed down her neck as gently as he'd ever kissed anything before.

"God..."

"Feels good?"

"Yes," she breathed.

His dark mind sought out the impossible. Her truth. There was something so wrong with her that if she hadn't wanted to be kissed and held before, he wanted her to see the light, the softness, and have that same reaction.

Maddy tilted her neck even as she leaned into him.

He bit her neck.

"God..."

His tongue lashed the bite mark. "No one should be without a kiss."

And in that moment, with her gyrating against his erection, he wanted to make her feel desire for *him*, not for just a kiss or sex. He stepped back, running his hands down her sides and resting them on the swell of her ass. Her eyes were heavy-lidded, her lips parted.

Maddy wasn't the enemy right now. She should have been disgusting and the definition of his degradation. But all Luke saw were big, beautiful eyes that fought too damn hard to hide the truth. She'd been hurt. As much as she might swear she created beautiful things for others, no one had created them for her. Or she hadn't let them.

On the isolated sidewalk from the musicians and artisans on the main drag, he cupped her cheeks and saw them flush. Just the touch of the drumbeats drifted in the night air as she watched him. He wanted her to anticipate what he would do, how it would feel. He wanted her to feel as alive as the city around them. He pressed his mouth to her full lips, and she sighed. The feeling went straight to his groin and made his heart tighten. Luke urged her mouth open, delving his tongue almost reverently.

She was hesitant, sweet, and tentative, but her fingers flexed into his biceps. She mimicked him, coming alive as much as he was. God, it was a helluva kiss. He backed her against the brick wall, running his hands into her silky hair, and kissed her forever. Slowly, he pulled back, eyes on her.

When her eyes finally opened, she blinked as though in a haze. "Wow."

The quiet word made him smile. He took her small hand. "Come with me."

They set off in silence the opposite way he'd been headed, passing trellises of vibrant flowers under the yellow street lights. The warm night and the crowd surrounded them as they surfaced back on the strip. Fruit stands. Musicians playing drums. Artisans hocking wears. Local eccentricities made him feel human, less like a warrior on a mission, and more like a man with just one purpose in life. Luke threw his arm in the air and hailed a taxi as it trolled for a fare. Immediately, it pulled a U-turn, honking at other cars that were rightfully where they should be, and pulled alongside the curb. He pulled the door open. "In you go."

Her eyebrow rose. "I can have a driver here in a minute, flat."

A grin curled his lips. "Nervous?"

"No."

"Then in you go. Time to get the princess out of her castle." A moment of beautiful surprise crossed her face, making him falter a step, though he *never* faltered. He also *never* spent time with skin peddlers, preferring to take them *out* than take them to dinner. Which was what he was doing.

He leaned to the cabbie. "You know where Cuba de Ayer is?"

The man nodded and jumped into traffic, but Maddy's finger began to wave. "No, no, no."

Luke leaned back, smiling. "What? Not hungry?"

"Not really," she replied with a nervousness he found endearing.

"You're having a hard time with the lack of control right now?"

"Um, yes." Her face tightened. "But—"

"Sit. Back."

Throwing her hair over her shoulder, she slipped back, eyes locked on him. "This isn't what I signed up for."

Luke ran a hand over his face before settling back. "Beautiful, me neither."

CHAPTER TEN

They breezed in and breezed out of the famous, open-all-night joint in Little Havana, and Maddy didn't say a word. Luke ordered to go, and she had no idea where they would go with Cuban takeout. The taxi had long since gone, and he took her arm, guiding her outside, helping her over a step.

"I've got it." She pulled away from the protective gesture. She didn't need anyone to cross a threshold covered in flowering vines. A midnight meal and a romantic Miami street might've been an ideal night out, but not for her. The tension in her shoulders was nearly killing her, making it hard to breathe and impossible to think. The only thing that would clear her mind was another kiss, and this guy—she couldn't stop replaying how his mouth had taken hers—wanted none of that. Apparently, he wanted *Masitas de Puerco Fritas*.

They rounded the block to an apartment building that had seen better days, and he dragged her like a gentleman up the brightly painted stairs and into the unit farthest away, in a corner that overlooked both the street and an alleyway. Her father would appreciate the thought that had gone into a unit placed like that.

As it did in any new location, her training kicked in. She quickly scouted the exits and knew the place well enough to map it out. Several things caught her vision that could be used in an escape, not that she was worried about leaving. Her precautionary measures were who she was.

The apartment was clean but barren. The walls were plain, the furniture sporadic, much in contrast to the streets of Little Havana.

A nondescript sofa and coffee table. A couple of lights. A small hallway led to what could only be assumed to be a bedroom and bath.

"This is your place?" His suit was custom tailored and expensive. It hung on his frame as if each stitch had been hand threaded with his physique in mind. The man didn't match his place. There were no hints of his law enforcement or military job—whatever it was that he did—which should have been enough to keep her away.

"Sort of." He threw the bag of takeout on the counter then turned, watching her stalk the room.

Nothing personal anywhere decorated a single square inch. The building hadn't seemed to be a flophouse. It was definitely nicer than that with the gardens and ornate gates. They weren't extravagant but tasteful and well-planned.

"Not what I expected from your place," she said.

"Not really *my* place." He shrugged. "Just a place."

Paranoia seeped into her. He'd kissed her but hadn't touched her since. Was it a setup? He brought her to a secluded location, without security or transportation. Even as she studied him, she couldn't believe that was true. But…why else was he going to eat a late dinner after he'd swept her off her feet? This was the problem with attraction, why there was an industry built on it. She was off her game, making stupid mistakes, just to get a fix of that insatiable feeling. "I'm going to head out."

Apparently done watching and waiting, he pushed from the counter. "Freeze, beautiful."

She obeyed. Her limbs shivered, and that thrill she chased so hard ran down her back. "Why?"

His long strides ate the space between them until his hands cupped her face, and he took her in a hard kiss. Before had been teasing, a whiff of his masculine scent, a tentative sample of what would come. But now, his mouth owned her. He forced her to submit, their tongues clashed, and she clawed her arms around him, clinging to what she wanted—him.

His hands climbed up her back, threading into her hair. His fingers knotted and pulled, making her moan. The light bites of pleasure were erotic, and her flesh jumped to life with the hot need of arousal.

Luke hugged her with one arm and bit her lip as he hustled them down the hall. The bedroom door bounced against the wall. She shut her eyes to focus on one sense at a time. Looking at him would be too much—until he tossed her on the bed. Then her eyes flew open.

The room was just as sparse as the front area. It was clean, almost sterile, making the man standing before her contrast harshly with their surroundings.

With strong, deft movements, he untied his tie and pulled off his jacket. A quick toss landed the jacket on the floor and the tie on the bed. He filled out his button-down shirt, his muscles bulging. Those biceps were a flex away from splitting the fabric, his chest a deep breath from popping the buttons. Slowly, his fingers unfastened each one, and he stripped the shirt to show the decadent artwork.

He took a condom out of his wallet and tossed it on the nightstand. "I don't want to hurt you."

She sucked a quick breath at the promise of sex. "You won't. I know you won't."

With a quick shake of his head, he stepped closer. His gaze ran the length of the black dress. "Why have you never been kissed?"

"I've never been interested."

His jaw flexed. "Why?"

"Nothing's wrong with me." But a million things were wrong with her. What woman made it to her twenties without ever experiencing arousal?

His head shook again. "Didn't say that. I was just wondering what happened or what it took."

"Just you," she whispered.

"Damn." Luke stared at her before he drew in a deep breath. "Tell me more. About you. About why. I want the truth."

She closed her eyes, shutting the world away, picturing his honest inquisition. He really wanted to know. This wasn't for a case. He wasn't building a file against her.

Without looking directly up, because she couldn't stomach if his face dropped in disgust, she swallowed a lump of guilt. "I never knew my mother and grew up with a deviant for a brother. He took after the monster who is our father." Maddy looked up to stare at what surely would be disgust. But it wasn't.

"You saw things you shouldn't?"

She nodded. "If that's what sex was, what arousal was, then from early on, I wanted nothing to do with it. The things I saw, heard…"

He came to her, and she rested her cheek against his chest while Luke stroked her hair.

Turning her head, she pressed her lips to his skin. "You're the first person to make me feel like I'm not in this fight alone."

"What fight?" he asked.

She tried not to shake as she readied to share another, maybe her most important, secret. "To take out Papa and crumble Mercier."

There. She'd said it to someone besides Hale. If Luke was a pawn for her father, testing her, then he would kill her. If he was a federal agent not on Mercier's payroll, then he'd use that info to get what he wanted. Instead, he pulled her to sit on the edge of the bed, sank to his knees, and pressed his perfect, soft lips to hers. The kiss was a promise, and she hoped that meant she'd eventually win her battle.

Her mouth stilled on his. "Please don't hurt me."

A careful, purposeful caress answered before he did. "No one has ever taken care of you."

"No."

"Time's come, beautiful."

He swept her onto her back, laying her across the mattress while his heavy weight came over her. Luke kissed her sweetly, as though he was trying to rid her mind of everything outside this room, as though he wanted to erase her world by making her feel so light and airy that she was melting and flying at the same time.

His hands smoothed against her sides, taking his time as he explored. "Sexy dress."

"It unzips." Maddy twisted, and Luke dragged the zipper down slowly, letting his fingers trail down her back. Her skin erupted in shivers. An addictive rush ran down her spine as he bent to kiss one shoulder blade, slipping the dress off.

"Oh…" She couldn't think with his tongue and teeth tracing a maze on her back. Maddy shimmied out of her dress and watched him take in the black bra and panties. "What?"

He smiled. "No joke, no line. I've never seen a woman as gorgeous as you."

A blush hit her cheeks, and before she could think of something that sounded better than a generic thank you, he took her lips while unfastening her bra.

Luke trailed wet kisses down her neck. "Just when I thought you couldn't be more perfect..." His hands tugged her underwear off. "But you are."

"Not at all." She shook her head. "I'm broken on the inside."

"Beautiful"—he held her gaze—"even if you are—broken—those things heal."

"I don't—"

"Trust me, I wouldn't have believed it. But they do."

Lying naked for him, baring her body and soul, she asked, "You've healed?"

"No." He leaned over, caging his forearms around her head. "But since I met you, I've realized that it's a possibility."

As his breath tickled her skin, Maddy closed her eyes, hoping that was true. She ran her hands down his corded back and stopped at his slacks.

"Take these off."

"Only because you're used to getting your way." He kissed her cheek, rolled to the side, and stripped.

"Luke..." He was magnificent. Given her life, she'd seen naked men before, but none as broad and defined. His thick length unnerved her, and she had no idea how...*this* would, could, happen. Her gaze trailed over his shaft and rose over the definition of his abs and the ink on his chest, to the chiseled face watching her take him in.

"You okay?"

She nodded. "Better than." But worried about his size, how it would feel. Worried about a thousand awful things she'd come to expect with sex.

Luke moved to her, holding her, kissing her, making her entire body light up. His fingers were feather light, his mouth blazing hot. His strong hands massaged her breasts, explored her stomach and her hips, then dipped further south. She pulsed in want and became slick with need. He was *readying* her, and, God, that made her want him even more.

As his fingers slid between her legs, she waited for the incredible sensation to go away, for it to hurt. But Luke stroked her as languidly as he kissed her, gently urging her thighs to spread, and then teased her folds open, paying deliriously amazing attention to her sweet spot.

"Feel good?"

"Yes," she whispered, shocked and hungry for his further seductive onslaught.

One long finger moved inside her, and her eyes rolled back.

"Still?"

"Still." Her breathing hitched at the intrusion. Wanting more, her hips rocked, and he used two fingers, stretching her, making her feel delirious. "God."

He growled against her neck as he kissed. His hand thrummed into her tightness, and his thumb encircled that spot where he'd started. "Never been kissed. Never been touched."

She nodded her head, her shallow, rapid breaths rasping. A building tension ran from her shoulders to her mound. She wanted to scream for more but also to push away and run from whatever was coming. However, it was too good, too much—too everything she didn't know existed.

"Never come?"

"No," she breathed, and a thought hit her—he knew when her climax would come before she did.

The intensity of his touch increased. "Not even for yourself?"

"No. God…"

"Maddy." He took her mouth and worked between her legs.

Her sex almost hurt for needing relief. Her lungs were on fire, and she was lost in sensation, wanting more of what he was doing to her. "I'm—" She moaned. "Oh, Luke."

It was too much, and it would never stop. As though she was tightening and exploding, she clenched his fingers inside her body, and her eyes squeezed shut. A wave of euphoria hit her. It rolled through her with more punch than she could ever have imagined. Her feminine muscles spasmed, clutching his fingers, and she gasped his name again.

Luke stilled his touch and softened his kiss as though he knew the slightest movement to her oversensitive skin would be too much. Carefully, he moved, hugging her to his muscular frame.

"You good, beautiful?"

She was limp and lazy, her mind spiraling toward a sated oblivion that was nothing like what she knew of sex and orgasm.

"Maddy, baby. You're good?"

"*Oui.*" The French slipped out of her unguarded mouth without hesitation.

"Good." His brilliant smile lit the room. "What do you need from me?"

"That was spectacular."

He chuckled, kissing her bare shoulder. "We have a good thing."

"I want more."

His jaw flexed as though he was holding himself back. "Tell me."

"I need to feel you inside me."

The fire and hunger in his eyes jumped, but he didn't move. "Yeah?"

"Yes."

Luke took her hand and placed it on his shaft. He was hard, yet the touch of his hot flesh was shockingly smooth. Maddy stroked his length, watching how the movement changed his face. His eyes sank shut, his jaw tightening.

"What do you need from me?" she asked his question back. She knew what girls were trained for, what they endured, what they didn't mind, but she didn't know what free will should mean. The possibilities seemed endless.

"Anything, baby."

Anything... What did she want?

She took her time, dipping her head to taste him. Her tongue swirled around his crown, her thumb tracing the ridge on her upward stroke. A salty, heady flavor made her dizzy with want as she bobbed her head and held him with both fists. The sounds he made, the way he moved...it wasn't what she'd expected. This was *not* angry or dirty or degrading. It was freeing.

"Not going to come in your mouth," he ground out.

She stopped, pulling back. "Not what you like?"

"When you make me come, I want to be deep inside your tight pussy."

Oh. That was a good thing, and again, he made her shiver with excitement and even acceptance. "Okay."

Luke leaned over, tore the condom packet open, and slid it on. Her nerves picked back up, eyeing his size.

He touched her chin, directing her face upward. "Trust me to be careful with you?"

"*Oui.*" No question.

Luke laid her back as though she was precious. "Eyes on me."

"Okay." She obeyed, and his broad shoulders leaned over her, his heavy erection lying at the apex of her thighs. Her erratic breathing mirrored his, and that he was acting anything like she was...that meant something to her.

Maddy spread her legs, loving the light scratch of the hair on his thighs against her smooth skin. Together, they positioned him at her entrance.

"Put your arms around me," he growled and kissed her neck.

Nervous and anticipatory, she did as he asked. One of his hands continued to guide his erection as he carried his weight on the forearm by her shoulder. His blunt head pressed, both uncomfortable and not nearly enough. She tilted her hips as Luke inched inside her body.

"Baby?" His muscles trembled. Restraint colored his voice.

"Yes."

"Good?"

"God, yes." Hers was a pleading, a needy searching for more of him.

Luke flexed into her, inching again, slowly. The thickness was soul splitting. Her jaw dropped, her body arching. Everything from her mind to her body tightened.

"Relax, Maddy," he whispered.

But she didn't want to relax. She needed to feel it all. Maddy let him roll into her body, both enjoyable and painful, and she arched into the hurt.

"Hang on, baby," he growled like he was aching too. "Hold me tight."

She clung as he thrust. "Luke!" A sear of pain ripped through her that was so beautiful, so addictive that she prayed he would make that happen again.

"Maddy, tell me you're good." His lips pressed to her ear as he stilled deep inside her.

"Better than." In more ways than she could comprehend.

With that, he slowly withdrew and repeated that insane thrust, the one that consumed her, making her believe in miracles. The intensity was more than she could have dreamed.

As Luke continued, his hips keeping the rhythm, her body adjusting to the intrusion, she moaned and kissed and held onto the only man who had ever made her feel. This was something, someone, she never wanted to let go of.

The slow start of a climax caught her off guard. With all of the newness, she hadn't thought about what more could happen. But the tightening was out of her control, the need for more had her bucking into him.

"Damn, beautiful," he ground out. "Can't hold on."

But he didn't have to. She fell over the edge, completely out of control, holding on as the stars and the moon detonated behind her closed eyes. Luke groaned, his body stilled, and he strained in her arms as his orgasm hit him.

This wasn't deviant or dirty or disgusting. Sex with Luke Brenner was special, and as he collapsed on top of her, his breaths running the same pace as hers, she felt that way too.

CHAPTER ELEVEN

Luke scooped Maddy into his arms and walked to the bathroom. "It's not the Mira House, but it's still clean and hot."

He spun around the woman in his arms. He had given her what she wanted in bed and had taken what he needed, but his chest ached. Sex wasn't the fix he craved right now. What was it? Helping her take out her father and Mercier? That was a given goal of his, but somehow it felt heavier, as though he needed it more than he had an hour ago.

He put a towel on the counter then set her atop it, ditching the condom and turning the shower on to blast. Quickly, the small room began to steam, and he tested the water with his hand before scooping her back up and stepping into the spray.

The water wasn't too hot, but still she arched into his hold, and he kissed her sweetly as he slowly placed her on her feet. Her hair flattened against her shoulders, and her makeup washed away. She ran her fingers under her eyes to sweep away the smudges, instead only controlling the smear of black.

Her hair slipped over her shoulder, water dripping down. Luke pressed it away, taking an extra second to appreciate the softness of her skin. "You are so damn beautiful, you know that?" Water splashed off his chest, raining down on Maddy. "It's not just—" Why was he even talking? The woman made him stupid.

She closed her eyes and shook her head under the water. Wiping her face again, she blinked away the droplets on her dark eyelashes. "I was a sure thing. You don't have to keep up the lines."

That was the reason he needed to tell what was in his head. She was too convinced that everything was a façade, that he was still the enemy, but for him, they'd changed. Instead of trying to find the words, he let his mouth drift over hers. He tasted her kiss, teasing her tongue. His fingers kneaded into her back, and as she moaned, he dropped to her neck to feel her vibrations.

"Luke, thank you for this. But you don't have to."

"Your entire life, you've been told sex is a commodity." Taking more care, he lathered the soap between his hands and ran the sudsy bubbles across her body. He worshipped every curve, every swell, appreciating the smoothness that could only be described as extraordinarily feminine. "It is sometimes, but not all the time."

She shook her head slightly, but her eyes were closed. His hands ran the length of her, exploring and whisking away soap remnants until he held her close and their eyes locked. Her pebbled nipples pressed to his chest, her pouty lips kiss-swollen. Everything about her made him hard as steel again, yet he didn't want to fuck her against the wall—no cold tiles and hot shower spray surrounding their bodies. He wanted to take her like a man, to make her feel the million ways he knew he could make her moan, make her gasp. He wanted to make love to her until they couldn't breathe, to hold her until she refused to let go.

She was worth so much more than she realized. Everything he'd seen on the surface was all a front. Just like his pain addiction hid his hurt, her focus derailed everything else in her life. Luke wanted to make this one woman feel better, a direct contradiction to *his* only focus, his long-ago-lost girlfriend.

None of this made sense, except that part of him had staked claim to Maddy, and he didn't know what to do about that.

* * * *

The sweetness she'd never seen in the fighter before her was almost contagious. It almost made her feel as though her shell of a heart, held together with barbed wire, had softened. Maddy sighed, inching closer to him as Luke turned the water off. He stepped them out and towel-dried her body as though she were priceless.

This magnificent man made of etched, powerful muscle was

more than he let on. Not just a fighter. Not just an enforcer. He was...different, and he made her curious about what else she could experience with him, what she could give him to reciprocate what he'd done for her.

She wanted sex and fulfillment again and was falling for him. Such a problem. She'd said too much. Hours had passed, and it was time to go. "That was great, but——"

He caught her mouth, kissing her silent and awakening that warmness that bled in her veins. It was more than a ravenous desire for him to bring her to the edge. It was a happiness, a need to stay in his arms.

"You hungry?" he asked.

"No."

"I am." With his arms around her, Luke led her to the bed. "Lie down." He stripped the damp towel from around her, taking a long glance before pulling a sheet over her. "You good, baby?"

Nodding, she had no words because, no, she wasn't okay. Their connection was more than she'd signed up for and more than her mind wanted to handle, but she couldn't run away.

"All right, I'm past due on a phone call to work. Be back in a minute." He pulled on a pair of shorts from a dresser and left her alone. The sounds of him unwrapping his middle-of-the-night fried pork dish and mumbling on the phone reminded her of how they'd met. They were enemies. Yet here she lay.

She could wonder who he was speaking to or, again, if this was a setup. But a realization dawned *again*—she trusted him not to screw her, just as she had placed her faith in him when she said she wanted Mercier to crumble.

A few minutes later, the sound of takeout being thrown away and then Luke brushing his teeth in the bathroom made her skin tingle. She was eager for his return, anticipating his moves. As he walked into the room, she pushed up on an elbow. "Hi."

His dark eyes shone as he stalked to the bed. He leaned over, burying his head in his hands as though he couldn't figure out what the hell they were doing either, but then his body shifted. With a quick tug, the sheet pulled off of her torso, baring her hip. His hand ran the length of her, from thigh to ribs, in a sinfully slow move. He bent, placing a chaste kiss on her hip as his fingers froze in place, splaying as though marking ownership.

She *knew* ownership. It wasn't what she ever wanted or needed. But this, this feeling of belonging to someone, with the sparks and the sizzle, was a feeling she wanted to feel again and again. She remembered when he'd threatened her with handcuffs, when she'd alluded to the truth about what she wanted with Mercier. "When did you stop hating me?"

His teeth nibbled before kissing her side. "I don't know."

"We're not enemies."

"Not even close, and I'm going to make love to you, seeing as I can't stop thinking about you." His fingers flittered over her breast. The sensation was amazing. "There you go, beautiful. Give me your eyes."

She hadn't realized they were shut. And when she opened them, she saw the emotion on his face that she felt inside her chest, and she knew she was gone for him. Maddy let her fingers drift over him as their eyes stayed locked. "I don't understand why this is happening."

"Does there have to be a reason?"

She nodded, embracing the zings of excitement sparking through her body and embracing the soreness from their time in bed before. "In my world, yes."

"Too bad." His lips upturned. "I'm ignoring my world for you."

Her heart slammed within her. They'd just had explosive sex. Why did she want this again so soon? She was sore and had never had an interest before, but Luke had changed her from the inside.

His lips landed on her as he rolled her onto her back. He kissed her stomach, dreamily letting his tongue sweep across her skin. Her nipples hardened, and his greedy hands found their mark, massaging in a gentle way that made her want to cry. She embraced the softness, the man that was spinning her mind a million ways.

His hand went between her legs, and she moaned.

"Fuck, you can't. Can you? You're hurting?"

"No," she promised. "I can. Don't stop."

"Don't do this for me, Maddy."

"I'm not. Or..." Because, yes, she wanted him to need her, but she needed him the same. "Please."

"Beautiful." He swept hair off her face, then pulled away to find a condom and sheathe himself before returning to the bed.

Again, she was able to take in how hard yet gorgeous he was. His sexiest attribute, though, was the hungry desire in his eyes.

Slowly, he positioned over her, again one arm holding himself, the other grasping her hand. Their fingers interlocked, and he squeezed. As his lips found hers, he pressed against her ready entrance.

"Oh, God." She winced and kissed him, scared he would stop.

Luke's hips flexed, slowly filling her body as he urged her mouth open. The full feeling was deliciously tender, intentionally torturous, and unlike anything she might have expected.

"I," she breathed into his kiss, "need…"

He shushed her quiet, slowly thrusting his shaft into her, inching in deeper each time. "Beautiful, I've got you."

And he did. How it happened, she had no idea. But he held her, and he saved her from a world that had her captive. With his full length inside her, her head rolled back, and her body arched. "God, Luke."

He held her close then rode her slowly, in and out, hands locked together, eyes locked. The building sensation was intoxicating as two hundred pounds of ripped muscle dedicated its every move to making her body come alive.

The whirlwind of tightening muscles and uncontrolled passion blinded her. She was so close but couldn't fall. His teeth caught her bottom lip. The bite was so sweet yet so hard. He bit and sucked, his hips racing and flexing against her. Maddy crawled her legs around his hips, and with all of the force she'd expected to be fucked with, Luke made love to her. The intensity was ferocious. She couldn't breathe. His hard breaths tangled with hers.

"*Mon nounours*," she moaned.

His mouth dropped to her neck, and he devoured the sensitive skin, growling as they both found release together. Her climax made the world fade. No sounds, no sights. Just the overwhelming, addictive feeling of falling in love with him. He was her savior in so many ways.

Their bodies pressed together as he collapsed, spent and exhausted. Still, he held tight, and she didn't want to be let go.

CHAPTER TWELVE

The jarring phone ring pulled Luke from his coma-like connection with the woman in his arms. This moment, this night, had been unexpected, and he didn't want reality to come crashing upon them. As soon as it did, he would have to own up to who he was and why their paths had crossed. What did he want? To save her? To claim her?

Yes.

On so many levels, yes. Despite the turmoil inside his chest.

"Do you have to get that?" she purred against his neck.

Nodding, Luke shifted and pulled the covers around her. The phone stopped ringing, but he knew it would begin again shortly. He stalked toward the phone. Sure enough, the ringing restarted.

The screen read Cade. Of course it did. "Yo."

"Been off the grid long enough to work?"

Nowhere near long enough. "Got something for me, or you just bustin' my balls?"

"That woman you can't get enough of? She has a shipment outgoing noon tomorrow."

"Bullshit." The automatic reaction should have stayed silent. No need to give away how much he'd screwed up the investigation, nor did he believe the lithe beauty lying in his flophouse apartment had a major deal going down in less than twelve hours.

"Excuse me?"

"I'm just saying, maybe we're looking at this wrong."

"Shit, are you kidding me?"

"What?"

"You've fallen for her? Believing BS lies and pillow talk?"

Hell yes, he'd fallen for her. Claiming that could be a career ender. Ignoring their connection would be ludicrous. And where was she in any of this? She couldn't deny their chemistry. "What I'm telling you is there is more than what we see."

Her soft footsteps padded down the hall, and Luke turned to see her wrapped in a sheet. Her dark brown hair was tousled and framed her dangerous face. Her dark eyes danced, pleading with him not to bring reality into the shitty apartment while her lips readied an excuse to leave.

"How deep are you into this mess?" Cade asked.

"Deep, brother. I gotta go." Then he hung up the phone, tossing it onto the cheap, scarred counter. "You have a deal at noon?"

She didn't blink, but her business face morphed into place, taking away the sexy angel he'd just bedded, just loved. "We're not here to talk about that."

"You're here because I gave you what you couldn't get anywhere else. Ever."

Her lips pursed, and her hold on the sheet tightened.

Luke stalked closer. "You can't do it."

"What are you going to do? Arrest me?"

"You don't want that."

Her lips pressed together in a tight line. "Obviously."

He stepped closer, pulling her into his embrace. "There's something important here. With us."

"Don't—"

He hugged her. Held her. Pressed a kiss to the top of her head. "Yes. There is."

Maddy's body melted to his. "We're enemies. You said it yourself."

"Only because you want it to be like that." Time ticked by until he pulled her from his chest. "Why do you do it? You've said your lines, and I get that there's an underlying want to help them. But I've seen your soul and the walls you've put up."

"No." She shook her head too emphatically, her eyes shining with tears she was too proud or maybe scared to shed.

"Yes, beautiful."

Maddy pushed away, though he caught her in his arms. "Let go."

"Look at me." He swept her into his arms and carried her, the sheet trailing behind, back to the bedroom. "Why?"

"You wouldn't understand."

"Why?" he whispered.

"Luke!" She slapped her hands against his chest, pushing him away. "Stop."

"Why, Maddy? Tell me why you're hanging on to something so evil."

"Because I am evil!" She snatched the sheets against her chest. "And I don't want to be." Tears streamed down her face. "I was born into it, and I can bring it down. *I can!* But not now, not yet. He'll get away with too much, and he needs to pay."

"He, who?"

Her chin dropped. "My father."

"Maddy…"

She inched back. "I don't even know what you are, who you work for. I just know it's a detriment to what I live for."

"Those girls?"

Her head shot up, defiance in her eyes. "No. To kill him. One day, it will happen. It's what I need to justify my existence."

* * * *

"I can't let you murder your father." However, that almost didn't make sense, as much as Luke wanted to eradicate the world of filth. "Blood shouldn't do that to blood."

"Why not? He's done so much worse to me!"

"Maddy—"

"No. You don't know. You have no idea. I've been trained as a soldier my whole life. You saw me. I scaled a hotel wall of balconies. I stood by while he sold women."

"You said so yourself—you saved them as often as you could."

"Why are you making excuses for me?"

He pushed away. "I have no damn idea!" Pacing the room, he turned back. "But I am."

"That's crazy."

"This"—he pointed between them—"is crazy. Crazy and intense, and we'd be stupid to let it go just because you're scared."

"You are crazy. I'm a criminal. You're law enforcement." She threw her arms out. "I want to destroy my father's empire, not create some American press release where one person is taken off the streets!"

He pressed his hands to his temples. "Here's a story for you." Luke planted himself in front of her and watched her take him in. "Here's a press release for you."

Maddy's mouth opened, but nothing came out.

"I was seventeen years old and in love with the sweetest, greatest girl. My mom and her mom were best friends. We grew up together. We were *supposed* to live together forever. But one awful beach vacation, they took her. They, I now know, were the Rivera cartel. But by the time that intel came around, she was gone. I've dedicated my *entire* life to wiping out those who hurt her, and *nothing* has stopped me. Until I met you."

Bile churned in Luke's gut. Raw hatred flowed in his veins. Many years had passed. The pain was still eating him alive, but Maddy had somehow helped heal a wound that he thought would be forever torn open.

He took a step forward. "You've changed things."

"I'm sorry."

"I can't say how or why, but I can't let you go. I feel different because of you, and I won't let our pasts screw up what the future could be. I don't know what it holds. But I do know I sure as fuck can't walk away from you."

"I'm so confused by what I feel." Tears slipped down her cheeks. "I never *feel.*"

"Beautiful, I made love to you, and you felt it." He moved to her, pulling her against him. "And I'll do it again and again until you know you're worth it."

"I've fought for so long. To hurt Papa, to ruin his world. I wanted this for my whole life."

He kissed her forehead. "Work with me, let me help you with what you want, and be with me. There's something here to explore. We've gotta figure it out."

"It won't work. They'll arrest me. He'll just leave the country. I'll have a mark on my head unless he's gone and the whole cartel disabled."

"He'd kill his daughter?"

"I'm sure he killed my brother."

Luke's forehead pinched in thought until he took her chin in his hand and swiped her tears away. "If I can take care of those problems, if I can make sure you're protected, you'll try and stay by my side? I want what we don't have. Time."

Her eyes landed on his, and the emotional toll of sharing almost overwhelmed him. Maddy had a face for poker—he couldn't read which way she would go. One way, he knew she'd be his forever, as soon as they traversed the confused landscape of her tumultuous life. The other, he might never see her again unless it was to chase her down a cartel rabbit hole.

He *should* never see her again. Luke was addicted to pain, and not having the woman he wanted would be the ultimate pain. However, he hadn't felt that craving since their lives had intermingled. He didn't want to *hurt*. He wanted *her*. "Please, beautiful."

A soft sigh of acceptance escaped her lips, and he swung her into his arms as her mouth agreed, whispering against his ear.

CHAPTER THIRTEEN

"This is unorthodox." Cade ran a hand over his stubble-covered face but went back to whatever he was working on.

Luke had talked with both the task force team leader and Brock at Titan HQ, and they'd given him an earful of feedback. After running a summary of the discussion by Maddy, she'd agreed to meet Cade face to face and see if his idea would be a go. It'd either break open Mercier or ruin Luke's career, landing the woman he cared about behind bars.

He held Maddy's hand in the makeshift war room. Almost all the men had uncertain eyes on them, and he couldn't blame them. "This is Maddy Mercier."

A few unsteady nods came their way. Grayson seemed the most receptive, Javier the most on guard. Colin and Ryder simply stared.

"She's here to play ball," he continued.

Maddy moved closer to his side. "As best I can."

Cade's brows pinched, his gaze bouncing between her and Luke. "We do this, we do it my way."

Luke stepped forward, his boot in front of her high heel. "A few conditions, then we're a go."

The task force leader stood to his full height. They were matched for size and brawn. "I don't think so."

"She needs immunity. Protection. She gets that, we get everything she knows about her father and the Mercier cartel and their business partners. The task force has high-quality, actionable intel. It's win-win for everyone."

"Win-win," Cade repeated. "Bullshit. This does nothing for you."

"I've put my shit to rest." And he had. Somewhat. That was the direction he was going, and having talked to Brock about his anger and hurt, his need to chase an impossible answer, Luke had only one thought. "This is what I need."

He'd never discover what had happened so many years before. Long ago, he learned there would never be a body, and tonight he'd come to grips that he'd be without additional intel from the Riveras. But he could keep that heartache of losing a loved one to a cartel from wrecking others.

"That's it?" Cade scrutinized Maddy. "One woman will change everything you've been harboring and hunting?"

Luke squeezed her hand. "When it's the right woman, yeah."

She leaned into him. "I know, in your world, I'm not trustworthy. But in mine? My word is the law. I won't feed you lies, and yes, I have personal reasons for agreeing to help you—both in and out of this room." Maddy let go of his hand. "Take a chance on me. You've got"—she checked her watch—"two hours, and it's not just intel on Mercier. It's actionable on Suarez, Rivera, and Eastern European business partners. Instead of guessing your next move, listen to what I have to say then *know* what you need to do. Win-win."

Luke's heart was frozen in place. "Rivera?"

Cade crossed his arms, ignoring him. "And you're, what, just going to be some model-agency owner? No moonlighting Mercier act?"

"That's what I'm offering."

Cade's eyes fastened onto hers for what felt like eternity. "You're taking a hell of a chance on our boy, you know that, Ms. Mercier?"

Interesting wording from Cade. The hardass had a heart. Maddy didn't notice and nodded. Cade nodded back. No one followed up on her Rivera mention.

She squared her shoulders. "Turns out, a chance isn't what I needed—rather another perspective."

He couldn't wait another minute. Luke turned to her, knowing he had to ask and terrified that her answer would change everything. "What do you know about the Rivera cartel?" She blinked, studying him. He could feel his blood boiling, his headache coming. "Maddy. *What* do you know?"

She sank in on herself as though she knew the answer might be a game changer. "Where they buy, sell."

"I need to track someone down." His voice shook. His entire body needed to tremble, but he wouldn't allow that to happen. "Can you do it?"

"Bring my father down, you'll get a lot of information that might help. Product, placement, those things."

Products and placement? The words were his hell but also his salvation. He'd come to terms with wanting Madeleine Mercier more than intel on the Rivera cartel, but somehow she'd just offered him the world. *Fuck.* His heart pounded, and his mind raced. He'd been ready to put his hurt to rest, but now he was solidly excited about the future.

"Thank you." Luke folded his arms around her, not caring about a single guy in the room. "You have no idea."

"I'd say the same, but maybe you do."

He nodded and let her go. For the next twenty minutes, he listened as she schooled every federal agent in the room about an operation they thought they knew but really had no clue about. After she was done and they had scrapped and rehashed the new plan, she shakily moved to the back wall, watching Luke gear up with his team.

If all went according to plan, this operation would be over within a few hours. She'd be free, her father would be in custody in a way he could not wriggle his way out of, and she and Luke would no longer have barriers. They could explore away, both working on themselves. All she had to do was pull off her role in the setup.

* * * *

Maddy's clammy palms pressed against her designer dress. Nerves she would never admit to were eating her alive, which was ridiculous. All she had to do was walk into the warehouse, set Papa up, and be on her way. The room was stocked with well-hidden beefy men in gear, and as she watched her father's car roll into the main warehouse, she knew she never would have been able to enact a plan of this magnitude on her own.

Luke's team had subdued Papa's advance team. They always came in for a security sweep, but she was able to tell them how and what to say in order for Papa to believe everything was on course. They performed flawlessly, utilizing the two private security teams and law enforcement agencies that she'd learned had formed the task force.

The time had come for the door of the black Mercedes to open. She stepped forward from her vehicle, her father catching her eye.

"Madeleine." His smart suit said expensive, and he had his business face on.

"Papa." She walked forward, as confident as he had trained her, wondering if he could see through the traitorous bliss on her face.

As expected, the South American buyer's vehicle rolled into the lowly lit warehouse as well. Two men exited their car, briefcases filled with cash. Her father pulled her forward to the meet. She was a show pony of a daughter as much as his groomed next-in-line.

They spoke in Spanish, their already executed agreement solidified with a shake of the hand and—

"Freeze!"

Maddy jumped and screamed, even though she had known it would happen.

"Federal agents! Everyone, hands in the air! Hands in the air."

Where they'd hid and how they swarmed, Maddy had no idea. But the task force, dressed in full tactical gear, surrounded them. Voices yelled. They were pushed, and everyone went facedown. Her father, the bastard, never once reached for her, never checked her safety. No, he wanted to protect his product, his business, his way of life.

They were cuffed, Mirandized, and separated, all while she still waited for Papa to look at her with any emotion. Years of pent-up hurt teared in her stinging eyes and streamed down her face.

Harsh hands that she didn't know moved her out of the room. Her tears still fell, but the guilt she'd expected never showed.

As her father and the buyers were separated, an agent pulled her to a poorly lit hallway. "Wait here." He parked her on a bench, her hands cuffed behind her.

She was all alone until she heard the steady rhythm of boots coming for her. "Luke?"

He rounded the corner, and his eyes landed on hers. "Beautiful."

His hands cupped her cheeks, hauling her up to meet his kiss. Her eyes sank shut when he stopped kissing her, and he swiped the last remnants of her tears away. "You did great."

She sniffled.

"Are you okay?" he asked, spinning her around to remove the handcuffs.

Maddy nodded and rolled her wrists as she turned back. "Better than I expected. Thank you."

"Always with the gratitude." He kissed her again. "Not sure what you're thankful for this second, but I'll take it."

EPILOGUE

Two years later…

"Never, in a million years, did I think I would marry you."

Luke laughed, tossing his head back as they dangled their feet over the edge of the infinity pool in the penthouse suite of the Mira House. "You're telling me you thought you'd get married, just not to me?"

Maddy joined him in the laughter, leaning against him. The moon was high overhead. She took his other hand, pulling his forearm out so she could see the word *beautiful* newly tattooed on his skin. "What I thought was that I'd never have sex with you in this place after you walked out on me."

"The night's still young. We can always leave—"

She slapped his chest. "You better not play."

Kissing her quiet, her husband lifted her off the ground and carried her into the bedroom. "Ready for your wedding present?"

Still laughing, Maddy wrapped her arms around his neck. "I thought the sex was a given, not a present."

Luke's eyes danced as they both dropped onto the bed. He reached under a pillow and pulled out a nondescript black box with a simple silver ribbon. "Take it."

Maddy picked up the deceptively heavy box, watching him watch her, and then tugged it open. She pulled away a layer of tissue paper.

Handcuffs.

Excitement rushed through her as she remembered all their handcuff teases, and she tossed the box after pulling them out. They were *engraved* handcuffs with the word *Beautiful* etched on one side.

"So it's going to happen." She kissed him, wrapping her arms around his neck. "You're finally going to have a chance to cuff me."

"Definitely going to happen." His chest rumbled as he kissed her back.

It was perfect. In the suite where it had all started, reminding her of where they'd come when she promised him he'd never restrain her.

"Hands above your head, baby."

One cuff clinked around her wrist. Then the other. She smiled as she complied. "*Je t'aime.*"

He hauled her back to the headboard. "Love you, too."

The End

Sign up for the 1001 Dark Nights Newsletter
and be entered to win a Tiffany Lock necklace.

There's a contest every quarter!

Go to www.1001DarkNights.com to subscribe.

DISCOVER THE LILIANA HART MACKENZIE FAMILY COLLECTION

Trouble Maker
A MacKenzie Family Novel
by Liliana Hart

Marnie Whitlock has never known what it's like to be normal. She and her family moved from place to place, hiding from reporters and psychologists, all because of her gift. A curse was more like it. Seeing a victim, feeling his pain as the last of his life ebbed away, and being helpless to save him. It was torture. And then one day it disappeared and she was free. Until those who hunted her for her gift tried to kill her. And then the gift came back with a vengeance.

Beckett Hamilton leads a simple life. His ranch is profitable and a legacy he'll be proud to pass onto his children one day, work fills his time from sunup to sundown, and his romances are short and sweet. He wouldn't have it any other way. And then he runs into quiet and reserved Marnie Whitlock just after she moves to town. She intrigues him like no woman ever has. And she's hiding something. His hope is that she begins to trust him before it's too late.

* * * *

Rush
A MacKenzie Family Novella
by Robin Covington

From Liliana Hart's New York Times bestselling MacKenzie family comes a new story by USA Today bestselling author Robin Covington...

Atticus Rush doesn't really like people. Years in Special Ops and law enforcement showed him the worst of humanity, making his mountain hideaway the ideal place to live. But when his colleagues at MacKenzie Security need him to save the kidnapped young daughter of a U.S. Senator, he'll do it, even if it means working with the woman who broke his heart … his ex-wife.

Lady Olivia Rutledge-Cairn likes to steal things. Raised with a silver spoon and the glass slipper she spent years cultivating a cadre of acquaintances in the highest places. She parlayed her natural gift for theft into a career of locating and illegally retrieving hard-to-find items of value for the ridiculously wealthy. Rush was the one man who tempted her to change her ways…until he caught her and threatened to turn her in.

MacKenzie Security has vowed to save the girl. Olivia can find anything or anyone. Rush can get anyone out. As the clock winds down on the girl's life, can they fight the past, a ruthless madman and their explosive passion to get the job done?

* * * *

Bullet Proof
A MacKenzie Family Novella
by Avery Flynn

"Being one of the good guys is not my thing."

Bianca Sutherland isn't at an exclusive Eyes-Wide-Shut style orgy for the orgasms. She's there because the only clue to her friend's disappearance is a photo of a painting hanging somewhere in Bisu Manor. Determined to find her missing friend when no one else will, she expects trouble when she cons her way into the party—but not in the form of a so-hot-he-turns-your-panties-to-ash former boxer.

Taz Hazard's only concern is looking out for himself and he has no intention of changing his ways until he finds sexy-as-sin

Bianca at the most notorious mansion in Ft. Worth. Now, he's tangled up in a missing person case tied into a powerful new drug about to flood the streets, if they can't find a way to stop it before it's too late. Taking on a drug cartel isn't safe, but when passion ignites between them Taz and Bianca discover their hearts aren't bulletproof either.

* * * *

Deep Trouble
A MacKenzie Family Novella
by Kimberly Kincaid

Bartender Kylie Walker went into the basement of The Corner Tavern for a box of cocktail napkins, but what she got was an eyeful of murder. Now she's on the run from a killer with connections, and one wrong step could be her last. Desperate to stay safe, Kylie calls the only person she trusts—her ex-Army Ranger brother. The only problem? He's two thousand miles away, and trouble is right outside her door.

Security specialist Devon Randolph might be rough and gruff, but he'll never turn down a friend in need, especially when that friend is the fellow Ranger who once saved his life. Devon may have secrets, but he's nearby, and he's got the skills to keep his buddy's sister safe...even if one look at brash, beautiful, Kylie makes him want to break all the rules.

Forced on the run, Kylie and Devon dodge bullets and bad guys, but they cannot fight the attraction burning between them. Yet the closer they grow, the higher the stakes become. Will they be able to outrun a brutal killer? Or will Devon's secrets tear them apart first?

* * * *

Desire & Ice
A MacKenzie Family Novella
by Christopher Rice

Danny Patterson isn't a teenager anymore. He's the newest and youngest sheriff's deputy in Surrender, Montana. A chance encounter with his former schoolteacher on the eve of the biggest snowstorm to hit Surrender in years shows him that some schoolboy crushes never fade. Sometimes they mature into grown-up desire.

It's been years since Eliza Brightwell set foot in Surrender. So why is she back now? And why does she seem like she's running from something? To solve this mystery, Danny disobeys a direct order from Sheriff Cooper MacKenzie and sets out into a fierce blizzard, where his courage and his desire might be the only things capable of saving Eliza from a dark force out of her own past.

1001 Dark Nights

Welcome to 1001 Dark Nights… a collection of novellas that are breathtakingly sexy and magically romantic. Some are paranormal, some are erotic. Each and every one is compelling and page turning.

Inspired by the exotic tales of The Arabian Nights, 1001 Dark Nights features *New York Times* and *USA Today* bestselling authors.

In the original, Scheherazade desperately attempts to entertain her husband, the King of Persia, with nightly stories so that he will postpone her execution.

In our versions, month after month, each of our fabulous authors puts a unique spin on the premise and creates a tale that a new Scheherazade tells long into the dark, dark night.

For more information, visit www.1001DarkNights.com

ABOUT CRISTIN HARBER

Cristin Harber is a *New York Times* and *USA Today* bestselling romance author. She writes steamy new adult, romantic suspense, and military romance. Readers voted her onto Amazon's Top Picks for Debut Romance Authors in 2013, and her debut Titan series was both a #1 romantic suspense and military romance bestseller.

Stay in touch for new release and exclusive info:

Newsletter: bit.ly/11aWFzM or text TITAN to 66866

Facebook page:
https://www.facebook.com/cristinharberauthor

Team Titan Facebook page:
https://www.facebook.com/groups/1411308265771683/

DELTA: RETRIBUTION
By Cristin Harber
Now Available

A MAN IS NOTHING

Trace Reeves was one bad day from a dishonorable discharge. The best the Navy SEALs had to offer, he became a vengeful, angry mess when his twin brother was killed-in-action. Now he's focused on a deadly obsession and unable to cope with the pain and guilt... except one time, in the arms of a one night stand that he'd never see again. She was smart, the sexiest thing he'd ever touched, but she disappeared into the night.

WITHOUT HIS TEAM

Titan Group was recruiting for their Delta team. They wanted ghosts. No ties. Nothing personal. The best of the best who could live off the grid and surface when commanded. Trace was the perfect recruit. Damaged. Heroic. Nothing to lose.

UNTIL A MISSION--OR A WOMAN--CHANGES EVERYTHING

But when Trace's one-time fling becomes his high-value target during a black ops job, the lines blur between her rescue mission and saving himself.

On behalf of 1001 Dark Nights,

Liz Berry and M.J. Rose would like to thank ~

Liliana Hart
Scott Silverii
Steve Berry
Doug Scofield
Kim Guidroz
Jillian Stein
InkSlinger PR
Asha Hossain
Kasi Alexander
Chris Graham
Pamela Jamison
Jessica Johns
Dylan Stockton
and Simon Lipskar

CPSIA information can be obtained at www.ICGtesting.com
Printed in the USA
LVOW12s0349150316

479097LV00001B/211/P

9 781942 299356